THE HERMIT

ALSO BY LOUISE WALTERS

THE HERMIT

Louise Walters

2022

Louise Walters Books

The Hermit
by Louise Walters
Copyright © Louise Walters 2022

The moral right of the author has been asserted according to the
Copyright, Designs and Patents Act 1988.

This is a work of fiction. Names, characters, businesses, places, events,
and incidents, are the product of the author's imagination or are used
in a fictitious manner. Any resemblance to actual persons, living or
dead, or actual events, is purely coincidental.

A catalogue card for this book is available from the British Library.
Produced and published in 2022 by Louise Walters Books
ISBN 978 1 7391095 0 9

Typeset in PT Serif by Louise Walters Books

louisewaltersbooks.co.uk
info@louisewaltersbooks.co.uk

Louise Walters Books
Northamptonshire
UK

For all those who love a novella

SATURDAY

It's the evening of a June day, the heat of summer turning in on itself. The bluebells have shrivelled. A blackbird sings. Long shadows creep across the valley. A kettle whistles and Theo crouches to make tea. He takes it in his enamel mug, without milk or sugar. Strong. A little turquoise car flits through the trees, bright and quick, like a kingfisher. The car emerges from the dense green, disappears for a moment behind the rhododendrons, then reappears, and he watches as it bumps slowly and steadfastly down the steep track towards the row of cottages. It draws to a neat halt outside the gate. The engine is switched off; the car gives a little shudder. It makes hot clicking noises. A pause follows during which nothing happens. Bees, out late. From the car two women emerge. The blackbird takes startled flight. One of the women is middle-aged, the other much younger. A teenager? It's hard to tell. They are mother and daughter. Any fool can see that, even an old one whose eyes are failing him. He takes it in his stride. He can sense, rather than see, the scowl decorating the teenager's face. But there's nothing wrong with scowling if that's what this world deserves.

1

The other woman looks hopeful. With a lurch he recognises the pale face, the slim build, the way she holds herself; and of course, the hair, undoubtedly this woman's crowning glory. The cold breath of regret blows across his neck. He is gripped by dread, unexpected, as he clutches the mug. Rich brown curls coil over her slim shoulders. Thick hair, beautiful. Her one concession to beauty.

He has to sit down. He trembles as he sips his tea. Dew falls. He tries not to think, and refuses to remember. He mustn't recall anything. He will be done for if it all comes back. Stiffly, he stands. He should go in. But he can't, not yet. He must keep watch.

He'd always thought she would not return.

She opens the boot of her neat little car and takes out luggage. So she is staying. Is this a holiday? Can it be? The daughter – for it must be so – offers no help. She looks across at him. He looks at her. They are far enough apart for him not to be certain their eyes have met, yet they are close enough to observe each other. He doesn't wave or nod, and neither does she. There's never been any call for him to acknowledge the visitors who come here.

'Carry these two for me, Antonia, would you?' says the older woman. And it is her. There is no doubt. Sylvia. She was a young woman the last time he saw her, fresh, pretty, innocent, stomping up the track. It was a relief, when she'd left. A broken link to memories he'd wanted buried.

Sylvia looks bitten and stumped. He shivers, long and cold, and grips his mug ever more tightly. Sylvia raises her hand in a half-wave. He nods, but it's too late to wave back. She has already looked away.

'Who is that man?' asks the young woman, her voice a mountain stream.

'Nobody important. Take this, please!'

The younger woman, for she is a woman, yet also a girl, sighs. 'Do I have to?'

'I can't be expected to do it all myself.'

Sylvia pushes open the gate, and they walk past the large kitchen window of the first of the three cottages in the row. At the porch, Sylvia puts down one of her suitcases and she knocks on the door. He watches, breathless. The woman Sylvia knocks again. The inner door opens. Yellow light floods the porch. He watches, and waits.

'Sylvia? I thought I heard a car!' And a tanned thin arm is flung out. They shake rigid hands. 'And is this... Antoinette?'

'Antonia.'

'My dear...!'

The teenager is not rigid, she melts into the frail arms like butter into a hot crumpet and soon both women are sucked in, they are in the house, pulled in by the thin arms that belong to Rosalie.

Minutes later all three emerge, Rosalie with a fob of keys. They straggle, three in a row, to the door of the middle cottage, and Rosalie fumbles for some time with the key in the lock.

'It's always been a bit stiff,' she explains. 'But you'll remember.'

'Yes. I do remember.'

He watches as eventually the door springs open, and Rosalie is swallowed by the dark, until the hall light is switched on. The other two also disappear into the cottage. A few minutes later Rosalie emerges, wishing the new arrivals, 'Goodnight, my dears.' She returns to her own cottage and shuts the door. He hears the lock slide across, the bottom bolt too. He breathes deeply.

He stands up, stretching, and studies the locked door for some time, then resumes his seat on the log. He lights his pipe, and smokes in quiet reflection, as the dew heavies around his feet, and the sun finally dips below the tree line. Calmer now. There's nothing he can do. Perhaps this was always going to happen, this return. This dredging.

The valley cools quickly even after the hottest days. He watches the cottages, the lights coming on one by one, as curtains are drawn, as figures move across blank and blinking windows. He imagines the explorations in one, the stillness and darkness in another, the tilted ambience in Rosalie's.

She has a house guest. A young man. An artist. Young. Too young, mercifully. But of course everybody is young now. Once upon a time a young man being anywhere near Rosalie would have driven him out of his mind, but not now, not this one, not quite.

The house is dark and cold, despite the heat of the day that's been. Sylvia remembers this smell: cottagey, ancient, animal. It hasn't changed.

Rosalie shows them where the light switches are, how the oven works, how to heat water. Sylvia is glad because she has forgotten these finer details. Is it the same oven? No. Not the same oven. More modern.

Rosalie says, 'Any problems, shout. I'm always around. And I do breakfast every morning, if you fancy it. I do it for all the guests these days. No extra charge, it's included in the rent.

4

Full English, pancakes, toast… excellent coffee too. Do pop around. About eight o'clock if that's acceptable?'

Sylvia glances at Antonia who shakes her head. No subtlety. Rosalie appears not to notice. 'The offer's there, no offence taken if you'd rather do your own thing. Goodnight, my dears.'

'I'm nipping out for a smoke,' says Sylvia. They have taken the rest of their luggage from the car and decided who is having which bedroom. Sylvia is in the larger of the three, at the front, looking out across the field towards Old Theo's hut. Antonia, who does not care for views, has opted for the bedroom at the back, next to the bathroom. The third bedroom, the smallest, will remain unused. Sylvia's been fiddling with the cooker. She's got the hang of it.

'I'll have a bath,' says Antonia.

'You may have to be patient with the hot water,' says Sylvia. 'It was always rather sluggish and I suspect it still is.'

'What does sluggish mean?'

'Slow.'

'Why are we here?'

'Why not?'

'But why?'

'For a holiday. I thought it would be nice to come back. You said you wanted to meet… your grandmother.'

'It's gonna be boring.'

'It's quiet. You're not used to that.'

'Is she really your mum?'

'Yes.'

'You're nothing like her.'

'Thank you.'

Antonia heads upstairs. Sylvia picks up her handbag, and she makes her way into the hallway, a yellow and hollow space that smells of dogs even though there are no dogs. It's dominated by the steep tatty staircase she remembers a guest once slipped down. He'd then threatened to sue (but didn't). She lifts the latch on the front door.

She sits beneath the kitchen window on an ageing wooden bench. There was always a bench here, but this isn't the same one. Things get replaced. She lights a cigarette and inhales deeply. She throws her bag on to the ground and looks over the garden, across at the field. The hermitage is still there. Of course. And the hermit is still there. Old Theo, sitting on his log, the embers of his fire descended into a low glow. She recalls the day she left. How long ago? Thirty years? More. Thirty-five? She was seventeen. *Work it out, Sylvia.* She has spoken to her mother three times in all those years. One call was to tell her Antonia had been born. Antonia was six months old when she'd called. Little interest was shown. The second call was to let her know Anthony had dumped her. The third was to book this holiday.

Sylvia, dragging hard on her cigarette, wonders if Old Theo still wears the same clothes. It was hard to see in the fading light when they arrived. In her memory he wore the one outfit. The tweed jacket, the – black? – corduroy trousers. The felt hat, indeterminate in colour, but so naturally blended with him and with his surroundings, it always seemed as though the hat had grown from his head.

Once, she had been aged ten or eleven, Sylvia had watched him wash his clothes in the brook at the bottom of the field. Then she had been intrigued as he'd draped them to dry on the

6

ground in front of his home. She had been fascinated, her customary listlessness relieved. He'd known she was there, of course, as she'd stood, motionless, watching him, but he'd ignored her; or he may have nodded.

He'd washed his body in the brook too. There was no bathroom in the hermitage. Probably there still isn't. She used to wonder where he went to toilet. Somewhere private, hidden in the woods. Is he a gypsy? A proper one, but without the travelling and the caravan? His hermitage, a hut, built by himself? When? Funny how you only question childhood things all these years later... nestled at the bottom of the field, backing on to the woods. Facing the cottages (Rose, Columbine, Bluebell), resolutely, and not without charm. His fairy tale dwelling, mysterious and frightening.

She drags on her cigarette. She holds the smoke in her lungs for a while. Then she exhales, slowly, luxuriantly. Smoking is her one great pleasure.

The hermit must enjoy a simple life, with nobody to confuse or wreck it. But who is he, truly? Theo. Theodore. Yes, but *who*? She'd not known as a child; had not asked. He was Old Theo, he was there. And the hut, his wood smoke, his pipe, his weathered face, his look of absolute resolution. She remembers the talk: *Once upon a time he'd been in love with a woman who'd betrayed him. He'd never got over it. There was a scandal... a fight... a falling out, a parting of the ways. A brother.*

A murder, some said. It was unclear. Rosalie had told her to ignore the gossip. All of it.

Antonia is quiet at the moment. She says little. Sylvia doubts she is worrying about her exam results. Her last exam was yesterday, and all day Sylvia had packed bags and cleaned

7

house, excited and nervous about taking this holiday with her daughter, their first alone together. Antonia has enjoyed annual foreign holidays with her father each August since the divorce, at first the two of them, then last year, with the girlfriend, Kelly-Marie. Antonia likes Kelly-Marie. She is "cool".

Antonia plans to go on to study A levels. English. History. Philosophy. It's a foreign language to Sylvia. Such subjects, such names. She has books. But she rarely reads them. There's no time, she tells herself. There's no time for anything other than work. Housekeeping. Tending to her plants on the balcony – almost gardening. Antonia, when she is there. Antonia when she is not there. There is no let-up. It may be different with sons. But she has no sons. She barely has a daughter. She flings her spent cigarette on to the floor. She obliterates the remains of it with a stab–twist of her foot. It's time to go to sleep. She'll get ready for bed once Antonia has had her bath. The long journey has tired her, she'll claim, and it won't actually be a lie. Antonia stays up late, she has done for the last couple of years. How does she get up for school each morning? Kelly-Marie has moved in. Perhaps she takes up a coffee for Antonia, a slice of toast, knocking patiently on her bedroom door.

Sylvia enters Columbine cottage, and turns to look across the field once more before closing the door. Was it wise to come here? Antonia had asked about Sylvia's childhood, or childhood home, many times since she was about six years old, showing curiosity, wanting to know about the almost mythical grandmother who Sylvia never spoke of. Then, in a quiet and rushed revelation, Sylvia knew she did want to show Antonia the places of her childhood: the valley, the cottages, the de-

8

lightful nearby seaside town where she had gone to school. It had come to her one morning, a fortnight ago. She had awoken with the conviction that she must return. And on impulse she had searched online and discovered the cottages were still holiday lets. She'd rang. Columbine cottage was free, miraculously. But, of course, it's still June.

'You won't find us much changed!' Rosalie had said. 'The twenty-first century is a rumour down here.'

There had never been a less maternal woman, and Sylvia's bad luck was to be her daughter. But she was no longer a daughter, Rosalie no longer a mother; one had been born, one had given birth. Accidental. Unplanned. Unwanted. Mutual. Father unknown. Never discussed.

Theo's hut is dark and still and silent, the fire finally reduced to a wisp of smoke floating up on the soft night breeze.

Sylvia closes the door, locks it, and heads upstairs.

SUNDAY

In the morning, Sylvia rises and opens the heavy, dusty curtains. Sunlight fills the room, and the valley, with bright optimistic light. It's around half past seven. She's never been one for lounging around in bed of a morning, even on holiday; *especially* on holiday. Antonia won't be up for at least two, more likely three or four, hours. Sylvia makes for the bathroom. The shower over the bath – both new – is feeble and lukewarm, but it's a shower; she steps out after many minutes of hair rinsing, refreshed and awake. There is no extractor fan, so she opens the window. Outside is the steep bank that had frightened her as child. She'd had visions of the bank, the earth, collapsing and falling on to the row of cottages. Of course she sees now it could not happen.

She dresses and goes downstairs. In the kitchen she boils water. She and Antonia brought a few provisions, a boxful of basics Sylvia had put away last night. But none of it appeals, so she makes her coffee – strong, black, like Daniel's – picks up her handbag and ventures outside.

She lights up and takes the first and best drag of the day, swiftly followed by her first sip of coffee. She sighs, stretches out her legs, and leans back heavily on the bench. This could be a good holiday for her and Antonia. The valley hasn't changed. The air feels the same, the trees look the same, the sky, the cottages, the hermit; older, superficially altered, but fundamentally unchanged. There's a peace to be found here, a feeling welcome and warm, despite her mother.

She is startled by Rosalie emerging from her cottage and vigorously shaking out a mat.

'There you are,' says Rosalie. 'Good morning!'

'And you,' says Sylvia.

'Did you sleep well? Were you comfortable?'

'I... yes, thank you.'

'Jolly good. Don't forget my breakfast, will you? I'm cooking soon. You and Antoinette are more than welcome to join us.'

Who might "us" be?

Does she fancy breakfast? It would be churlish to refuse. Of course, she is hungry. She is always hungry. Food often has no appeal for her. After she had left Devon, she'd skated perilously close to anorexia. Her concerned friend took her to a doctor, who told the teenaged Sylvia simply, in his avuncular tone, if she did not eat she would die. The words must have stuck because since then she has eaten, enough.

'I'll join you,' says Sylvia, 'but I'm afraid Antonia won't be awake for some time.'

'Fine. I'll see you in ten?'

She doesn't wait for an answer, but disappears back into the dark of Rose cottage. Sylvia stays on her bench for a few more moments and listens to all the noises of a breakfast in preparation. There is joy in the sound.

She's not sure whether to brush her teeth now or after

breakfast. She smells of cigarettes. She knows people dislike the smell. Yet she hates the taste of food when it's tainted with toothpaste. Picking up her handbag, she drains the rest of her coffee and goes back into the coolness of Columbine. She'll brush her teeth.

Sylvia taps lightly on Rose cottage's door, and is unheard. She clears her throat and licks her finger and wipes the corners of her mouth, in case there is any toothpaste residue. She forgot to check. She enters the cottage. There is no mirror in Rosalie's hallway. The kitchen door is open and she hears two voices, Rosalie's and a man's. She reaches the kitchen door and stands awkwardly, as the man at the table stops chewing and stares, for a moment. Then he resumes his chewing and waves his fork at her. He has the look of a wolf about him, arrogant and ruthless. Already she dislikes him.

'You are,' the wolf says, 'let me see... Antoinette?' His voice is deep, not unattractive.

'Come in, come in!' says Rosalie, turning from the large tatty stove. She waves a spatula.

Sylvia wearily regards the man seated at the table. He has black shiny hair. His clothes are dirty, drab, soiled with paint. He puts down his fork and holds out his hand as she sits on the bench opposite him. Sylvia allows him to take her hand. His skin is cold, taut.

'I'm Geoffrey Blackdown. I like to think of myself as an artist. But I suppose I could be viewed as a bit of a wastrel. It would be an easy mistake to make.'

She nods at the wolf man, withdraws her hand from the firm shake, and looks towards the large kitchen window. It

12

needs a wash. Rosalie says, 'Now, Geoffrey,' as she places a freshly-cooked golden pancake on to Sylvia's plate. 'Coffee?'

'Yes, please,' says Sylvia.

There's an uncertain silence as Rosalie pours coffee.

'Sylvia, Geoffrey *is* an artist. He's my guinea pig, actually. I'm thinking of offering retreats here for artists and writers. Bed and board, and converting the lean-to into a rustic-style studio. The owners are all for it.'

'That sounds... interesting,' says Sylvia, picking at the pancake. She takes a bite. It looks nice and smells nice, and even tastes nice, but she has no appetite.

'We've put sky lights in already,' says Rosalie, putting a pancake on Geoffrey's plate. He beams at her.

What could a rustic-style studio actually be?

'It needs a decent floor putting in and it will be fully usable.'

'I didn't notice when we arrived,' says Sylvia.

'You wouldn't, it was almost dark,' says Rosalie.

'I'll have to take a look at your work, Geoffrey,' says Sylvia. 'I'm certain it must be absorbing.' Geoffrey bows his head and winks. He looks closely at Sylvia, so much so that she shifts on the bench, and makes a point of looking away.

'Have you... haven't we...? Gosh, yes. I remember you. You're *the* Sylvia. Rosalie, you didn't say... I used to come here with my parents in the summer holidays. You were frightfully pretty. All that hair.'

She doesn't remember this Geoffrey. He regards her, bemused, amused, but she is in no mind to be friendly towards this man. He seems to hear her thoughts, and he nods at her, and looks away and continues to eat enthusiastically. Rosalie frowns at him. He smirks for a second or two, then his face clears, and takes on a new, softer expression.

'I say, I'm awfully sorry,' he says.

She can't tell if that's the way he naturally speaks or if he's putting it on. Either way he sounds affected and ridiculous, like some Agatha Christie toff.

'Look, Sylvia, I have an abrasive sense of humour. Feel free to ignore me.'

Sylvia resolves to, and looks again towards the large window where, despite the grime, sunlight pours in, unrestrained and jubilant. The garden gently slopes down to the hedge at the bottom, with a clear view across the small field to the hermitage. The smoke from the fire is dark against the morning sky. So he is up and breakfasting too.

The elaborate tattoo on Geoffrey's right forearm consists solely of the word YES. His eyes are blue, and his hair is almost blue in its blackness and sleekness. He is slim, tanned, and handsome, in the most unattractive way. Antonia will like him.

'So what do we have planned for today?' says Rosalie.

'I shall go out sketching this morning,' says Geoffrey. 'And I shall paint this afternoon. The studio is perfect, Rosalie.'

There is further chat, talk for talk's sake, and as soon as she finishes her coffee, Sylvia excuses herself. She slips through the gate between Rose and Columbine and sits down on the edge of the patio, which is a hotchpotch of ageing concrete slabs, which Sylvia supposes is also rustic. Stupid word. Pretentious. She lights a cigarette. The morning sun is balm to her skin, her mind. She is glad Antonia is unlikely to surface for a good while. By which time, the egregious Geoffrey will indeed be away sketching.

Rosalie is an extraordinary woman. There's a rare sort of energy about her, ageless and indefatigable. She could be any age between fifty and ninety. A woman of quick, vibrant movements; shrill of voice, but not harsh on the ears. Quick-minded too, Sylvia recalls. Yet she is not likeable. What a thing to know about your own mother. But facts are facts.

She works out that Rosalie is eighty-five. And she further works out that she left here, aged seventeen, in a fury, in despair, disgusted, disillusioned, once and for all, thirty-four years ago. Time. *Time.*

Theo washes his sinewy body. The water is cold. It's holy on his skin. Once a week, other than on the harshest of winter days, he submerges himself and washes all over. It's deep and wide enough here, in the bluebell wood, to provide a bath. He washes his face, neck, armpits, groin, feet. He is a clean man. Later he will wash some clothes. He needs new boots. He can't remember how long he has had this pair: many years. They are worn, the soles threatening holes. It is not what he wants to do, to request anything of her. But they have an understanding.

Returning to his hut, he looks up towards the cottages. The young woman is talking to the dark-haired young man. The girl is laughing. She is coquettish. They are at the door of the lean-to. The young man stands in the doorway, facing out, and he looks as though he would like to slam it shut and leave the girl standing alone and humiliated. At the same time, he looks as though he would like to eat her. And so, it begins again.

The artist fellow gives her a final little wave, a dismissal, and shuts the door on her. She stands, alone and motionless, and then looks around to make sure nobody has seen; and Theo, only too aware of how humiliation feels, quickly looks down at his worn out boots.

Later still, after lunch, he sees Sylvia sitting alone on the bench, smoking. He can't recall how many years ago she left. He knows the age of nobody, not even himself: he reckons he's about eighty-seven. And Sylvia must be in her forties or even her fifties by now. Her hair is starkly tied back today. It used to tumble down over her shoulders, her back, when she used to be pretty, when she was young. Later, as an older girl, her hair took on a horrible shape. The cut was all wrong. It has been years but she still has the look of— And the unframed idea sits rotten inside his gut.

She is too thin. Doubtless, with all this smoking, she eats little. She is troubled, by what, by whom, he can't imagine. But, yes, he can. Nobody truly escapes their roots. She is sad, obviously, and he wishes it were not so. She looks nice. Not many people do look nice, but she is one of them, and Theo feels a rush of protection towards her. Regret, too, until he remembers, and the regret vanishes, like youth.

The tent was small and striped, a cliché, but nevertheless, that's how it was. Helena Fenchurch, almost beautiful, elegant in her choice of clothes, fashionable, hovered outside the tent. She felt its allure, and she was wavering, knowing she was being silly. If she'd had a friend with her, that friend may have dragged her off, giggling, rightfully dissuading her from parting with her money. But poor Helena was friendless; there existed in her life a paucity of people in whom she felt she could

16

confide. That didn't exactly sadden her. Her life had always been so. Helena was mostly bored, and she lacked female company, that was all. As a child she'd had two older half-brothers. Now, as an adult, she had a husband and three sons. They were fine boys, no doubt, everybody agreed, everybody said so. And she was as proud of them as a mother should be. Her marriage was reasonable. As far as she knew, her husband was not unfaithful. Occasionally she would look upon other men wistfully, privately, wondering. There was… a man. One man. Infrequently seen, often missed. Her secret. Simon was a good man, essentially. Not astounding as a husband, not lacking particularly either. Wealthy, generous to her, and from the beginning he came complete with a beautiful home that over the years she had enjoyed decorating, furnishing, and inhabiting.

Helena had brought her boys to the travelling fair for a treat. They were under the watchful eye of their nanny, Agnes. Meredith was too old for a nanny of course, but Theodore and Clement still needed her, and so did Helena. Agnes was a good sensible woman, with nowhere else to go.

Helena had detached herself from them, telling Agnes to take the boys on to the carousel, and to let them take another turn each at the coconut shy. She would be a few minutes, Helena supposed. Agnes, cheerful, as fond of the boys as their mother was, happily obliged.

So, armed with the energy of rashness, when her turn came, Helena popped breathlessly inside the striped tent to hear her fortune. It was in the tea leaves. What nonsense. The tent was dark inside, and smelled of unwashed hair. Helena seated herself at the small table in the middle and looked uneasily around. There was not much to see: the dark canvas, the trampled grass underfoot, the "fortune teller" opposite her. The woman poured tea slowly, swirled it around in the cup, tipped it away, and silently studied the remains. Helena watched, bemused. What nonsense, but what fun. The woman held out her hand for payment.

'I see four children,' the fortune teller began after Helena had paid her fee. She was a young woman, earnestly staring deep into the tea cup. Helena had assumed such a person would be older, older than her, a crone, but this woman was about her age. Probably younger. It was unsettling, but she was there now, and she may as well go ahead with it, and hear her out. If nothing else, it would be entertaining.

'I have three children,' said Helena.

'But there are four, all together. Close, they are. Three boys and a girl.'

Will she…? Oh, did that mean, there would finally be a girl? Another baby to come? Her much-desired girl baby. Her Elizabeth, at last? The name she had chosen for Meredith, had he been a girl. Then for Theodore. But not for Clement.

She was glad Meredith was a boy, of course, the oldest child should be a boy, and he was fine, he'd been a bouncing baby, a bright child, who had become a handsome and unusually poised teenager. She had hoped Theodore would be her girl, six years younger than Meredith, but no, another boy, and so like his brother, they could be twins but for the years between them. Two fine boys, and Helena thought her family complete. And ten years after giving birth to Theodore, an unexpected conception. Not Simon's baby, of course; so as soon as she'd understood she was pregnant, she had engineered a night with her husband. They had used separate bedrooms for years. It al-

18

most didn't work, her engineering. Their sexless marriage, never discussed with anybody. Her secret too, never discussed, the baby's true father. It would go with her to the grave.

Helena did not enjoy pregnancy, and she certainly did not relish giving birth, any more than any woman of her sparse acquaintance did. It was a harsh torture, even if richly rewarded. She had hoped for a girl, of course, but she knew throughout her final pregnancy that she was carrying a third boy, so when Clement was born, she didn't even need to look or be told. Throughout the pregnancy, she didn't even think about naming the baby Elizabeth. Clement would be the child's name.

'I see happy children,' continued the young fortune teller, 'with all this world can give them. They are privileged.'

'Yes.' It was easy enough to gather that. Helena's clothes were of an obvious, undeniable, quality.

'The girl is... the sister... she is... adopted?'

'Adopted? No– oh!' It must be Rosalie. Not adopted, but patronised, cared for, and included, much of the time. Helena would not elaborate for this young woman though. Let her do the work. Let her prove herself.

'The sister is... is she a cousin? It isn't clear. But she's important.'

'Not important, no. I think you must be... seeing... our servants' little girl.'

'I see she is loved too much.'

'What on earth can you mean?'

The fortune teller – "Miss Zelah" – ignored Helena. 'I see there will be hard times ahead,' she continued. 'Tragedies.'

'What sort of tragedies?' said Helena, annoyed. There were

tragedies in all families, surely, to one degree or another. Nothing at all remarkable about that.

'I speak of death,' said the woman, quietly.

'Who will die?'

'All of us, m'am.'

'Yes, yes, I know. But... tell me what you see. Please. Be specific.'

'You shall outlive two of these children.'

'Outlive two of my children?' Helena was stunned to hear herself utter such words. But she was not surprised, or shocked, by this news. Miss Zelah's words were affirmation of her darkest fears.

'Yes. I'm sorry,' said Miss Zelah.

'Are you mad?'

'No, m'am. I see what I see.'

Helena stared at the calm young woman and she loathed her, sudden and pure, and she pushed herself up and away from the table.

'But that's terrible! Oh! What a horrid thing to say to a mother! You are a mean-spirited woman! Such bunkum!'

And Helena, crying, furious, picked up her handbag, her hat and gloves, and left the dark foul-smelling tent. What a stupid thing to do! What a waste of a florin! What nonsense! She wanted to see her boys, be with them. She headed for the carousel and was relieved to find little Clement sitting upfront on one of the gaily-coloured horses, and Agnes, ever careful of her charges, an arm looped around his waspish waist. Helena dried her eyes and smiled and waved at her children as they flew past and round, round and round, up and down.

And I can't help seeing what I see, thought Miss Zelah, whose real name was Susan; and she asked me to tell it, and I told it. And how much more, so much more, she had seen. Things not to be revealed. You nearly always had to keep something back. At least now the well-to-do woman had an idea. She could turn fortune around, be watchful, and protect her brood. The tea leaves revealed so much. It was a frightening art to excel in. Her mother had taught her. Looking into the cup again, she shook her head, and sighing, she swilled it out. She prepared it for her next visitor, now sitting eagerly opposite her, who, it would transpire, would have five girl babies (she currently had two) who would all outlive their mother, as it should be. One of the girls would not be quite right, slow of mind, and one hand would be withered, but whether right or left, Susan couldn't see, and she would not speak of it.

The first day full day is finally over, and it's evening time. It's been a typical first-day-of-the-holiday day. Sylvia allows herself to slump back into the soft sofa, her legs stretched out before her, flat and straight. She rotates her feet and examines her toes. They need a coat of polish. She could ask Antonia to paint them for her. Sylvia's opened a bottle of Soave. It's cheap and white but it's wine and it's nicely cold, and she takes small, tentative sips. She has done nothing all day. Smoking in the sunshine, "resting" after yesterday's drive down here. She'd pretended to read a book.

'Can we have a fire one night?' asks Antonia. She is lying on her belly on the old worn rug in front of the fireplace. It used

21

to be in Rose cottage. Sylvia used to lie on that rug too. It smells of feet, woollen socks, dust.

'Of course, darling,' says Sylvia. 'We'll need one, I expect. This warm weather won't last, it never does. The evenings can get chilly. Are you cold now, sweetheart?'

'No. I thought it would be nice, that's all.'

'We can fetch in some logs from the store in the shed.'

'How old do you think Geoffrey is?' Antonia takes a tress of her thick blond hair and curls it around her fingers, examining it.

'About forty, I suppose. He says he used to holiday here as a child, but I don't remember him. I remember a young boy visiting in the summer holidays with his rather arrogant parents, but I would never have recognised him.'

'People change, don't they?'

'Sometimes. Not always for the better. You should keep away from him. He's not a good person.'

'You are so judgemental!'

An owl hoots. It sounds close to the cottages. Antonia starts. 'What the fu–?'

'It's an owl. Tawny owl, I think.'

'It sounds like a ghost.'

The owl continues to hoot intermittently for several more minutes, and Antonia's initial alarm fades to boredom. She pushes herself up from the floor and yawns.

'Darling,' says Sylvia. She has to speak now before Antonia disappears upstairs and spends the rest of the evening in the bath.

'Yeah?' says Antonia, stretching.

'I hope... do you think we'll be able to talk about things?'

Antonia shrugs. 'I dunno. Depends what the "things" are. If it's about me coming to live with you, there's nothing to talk about.'

'I see. Another day, then. I think we do need to talk it through.'

'We talk it through all the time. Nothing's changed.'

Sylvia, her hand shaking, takes a sip of wine. She knew this would happen. But she has to try. 'You're tired, I can see,' she says, trying hard to smile. 'You go on up. There should be hot water. I popped the immersion on earlier. It's all a bit clanky, but it works.'

'The what?'

'Immersion tank. It heats up the water.'

Antonia reaches the lounge door and pulls it open. She stops halfway through and turns to Sylvia. 'Mum?'

'Yes?'

'Do you think Geoffrey has a girlfriend?'

Old Theo hasn't always lived as a mysterious eccentric in a hermit's hut in a corner of a forgotten field on his late father's estate. Once upon a time he was young and handsome, fit and strong, and rich, and in love. This last, is all that remains of the man he once was. All the other facets have fallen away from him, one by one, even the fitness. Yet he is a man who lives without regret. He has been described as creepy; crazy; psychotic; a recluse. None of these are strictly true. He is fabled by people who have never met him or even seen him. He is well-known "around these parts". The hermit in the valley. At Rowan Park. Rumours have it he lost his heart to a woman. They say she drove him mad. She betrayed him. No, he betrayed her. They say he murdered a man. His brother, wasn't it? They say. No, the brother died in the war. No, the other one. What other one? The younger one. Didn't he shoot himself? No, he *hung* himself. The hermit murdered *somebody*. Once. That's why he's a hermit, out of remorse.

These are the stories.

But Theo does not always regard himself as a murderer. He once lived in the big house at the bottom of the valley, Rowan House, white and grand and pillared; and he was once a second son: loved, bullied, hated.

And how he longed back then, and in the following years, for the wisdom of his older brother. Dead at the age of twenty-one. If only. There are no "if onlys"! There is only that which happens, everything else is imagination, and Theo knows that more than most. But why, *why*, did Meredith join up? He didn't have to, nobody would have thought any the less of him, fresh from university, a sparkling career before him in something or other, a life, and then that awful decision, right at the end of the war, and his mother collapsing as he told them, his father stoic: *Meredith is a man now, it has to be his decision*, and their mother crying, *No, no, you don't understand, Meredith, please think*, but Meredith would not think and he would not budge, his mind was made up, his short course in life was set. Theo, fifteen, newly handsome, standing alongside the window as the March sun feebly warmed his back, looking from each of his parents, to his older brother, and back again, saying nothing. He hated his mother's quivering fear. In the end, after Meredith left the room to prepare, for he was leaving that day, Theo picked Clem up off the floor, and the little boy would not let go of his red engine, and Theo held him close, and felt the

24

small boy's soft breath on his face. The red engine dug into both their chests, defiant and cumbersome, and for a long time Theo could not let his younger brother go. He stroked his head, over and over, his hair thick and clumpy.

If only (there are no if onlys), *if only* Meredith hadn't taken leave of his considerable senses, and joined up. Theo still ponders this, all these years later. Things would have been so different.

Sylvia has been perusing the bookshelves since Antonia went up for her bath. She can hear the water running, slow but sure, and she can hear her daughter singing to herself as she prepares for her ablutions. A sign. It means she's relaxed, doesn't it? Happy? Or in lust. Clearly Geoffrey has left the impression she feared he would.

There are many poetry books on the shelves. Some of the names she recognises, some she doesn't. Faded, tatty covers, obviously much-read. Faber poets. Larkin (who she actually recalls studying at school, and did enjoy).

Once, Daniel read poetry to her, as they soaked in a luxuriously hot bath. She had lost herself. It was their second night together. Every word had mattered, every nuance. But it had been false, and she'd known it even then, despite the ecstasy. Everything about Daniel had been false.

Antonia is in the bath. Sylvia hears the slosh of water. Time for a smoke. She turns away from the books. There's nothing for her on these shelves.

She wanders around in the garden, in sandals, her feet getting cold, the orange tip of her cigarette weaving around in the dark. Why she has come here, she does not know. Antonia. She is almost sixteen, this could be their last holiday together. Surely in sixth form she will find a boyfriend, and want to hang out with him next summer. Antonia has not yet had a proper boyfriend, remarkable in this day and age. About her there lingers an air of childhood innocence, cloying, and Sylvia vehemently wishes it gone. It's about time the girl understood things. Conversely, her dear daughter understands too much, in the manner of today's teens. But even so, Sylvia fears the power of this Geoffrey and she does not want him within feet of Antonia, who is already smitten with the black hair, the good looks. The attitude. The tattoo. Sylvia's teenaged self might have been taken with Geoffrey too.

Sylvia takes a long drag on her cigarette. There is no moon. The garden is peaceful. A tawny owl hoots; probably it's the same one that alarmed Antonia. Against the walls of Theo's hut, shadows of flame flicker in a night-time dance, and Sylvia imagines fairies carousing in the grass, fanning the flames. He is there, of course, Old Theo, hunched beside the fire, a darkened figure of indeterminate shape, still and silent, watching her, no doubt. He always *watched*. She cannot see his face, as he can certainly also not see hers, but she smiles at him, and waves, the glow of her cigarette trailing a bright arc across the black sky.

She has missed the solace of this corner of Devon: green, lush, and unworldly. The braying of the donkeys across the valley, the evening glow of Theo's fire, the blackness of the night sky, the uncountable country-sky stars. This is... it is home. It *was* home. Despite everything. She needed to come back, to face it. To talk to Antonia, to try to put things right.

Her feet are wet so she turns towards the cottage. It's not

26

been much of a day. It's time she went to bed. But she wants one more smoke before she turns in. She sits on the bench and lights up another cigarette. Chain-smoking hurts her throat. The strike and hiss of the match comfort her. The night is warm, and she is cloistered in the dark.

MONDAY

'I'm popping out for groceries today,' Rosalie announces. She is wearing a simple pink linen frock, with a cardigan a shade or two darker. It suits her, Sylvia concedes. The grey hair is washed and it's neat, short, shaped into her neck.

Antonia has managed to get up, wash, do her hair, and put on her make-up, all in time for Rosalie's complementary breakfast. The half-awake teenager sits alongside her mother on the bench, demurely picking at a pancake which Sylvia knows would be devoured in seconds if Geoffrey was not present. 'Would anyone like to join me?'

They all want to go. Antonia, because, Sylvia to buy a post-card and see the sea, Geoffrey, to try that little tavern at the head of the town. Good sea view. He'll stand lunch for every-body. He raises his eyebrows playfully at Antonia, who blushes and looks down into her black coffee.

'I say, Sylvia,' says Geoffrey, 'I brought a box of Merlot down here with me, courtesy of the old man. Would you like a couple of bottles?'

'No, thank you.'

'It is good,' says Rosalie. 'I'd take him up on the offer if I

28

were you.'

Geoffrey grins. 'I'll pop them round to you later.'

Sylvia offers to drive to town, an offer gratefully accepted. Rosalie has her own little car, and she still uses it to drive into Rowan Bay, for shopping and going to the doctor or dentist, but it would be a relief to be driven, she says. Sylvia's Fiat 500 (her post-divorce treat to herself. Something good comes of everything) is tiny, with not much room in the boot, she warns them. Driving is still fun and makes her feel free and alive, with "her" music blaring: Pearl Jam, Tori Amos, Nirvana, the air con blasting. She's young again when she drives, and a little bit reckless.

Rowan Bay is a small but busy town. Car parking is difficult but Rosalie knows and Sylvia remembers where to find the quietest car park, at the top of the town; a fair walk down to the shops and the sea front. Antonia complains. Nobody takes any notice.

In town they separate. They are to reconvene at midday for lunch in the seafront tavern. Antonia opts to grocery shop with Rosalie (*I'll show you around and you can carry the bags for me!*) and Sylvia wisely decides to say nothing about this, but to quietly allow it. The last thing she wants is a fuss, and how much harm could Antonia come to, wandering around in daylight hours in a bustling seaside town with an elderly lady? Besides, it's why they're here, isn't it? Antonia wanted to meet her grandmother.

Sylvia makes her way down to the beach for a bit of peace and to people-watch. Opposite the tavern a handsome young man has a tiny stand selling plastic flutes of Prosecco and cans of Coca-Cola. She opts for a Prosecco, and clutching the glass, she heads for the beach. She finds a spot, flings down her cardigan, and lowers herself, balancing the Prosecco. No sand here. Pebbles. Which she likes. She observes holidaymakers, tentative and laughing in little wooden pleasure boats, and straggling fishermen, in more serious mood, still tidying up after the morning's catch. The hot sun, blue sky, waves, relentless, pulling, pushing, for ever, on and on. It's idyllic, this moment, this hot day, these sounds of waves and seagulls and the hapless shouts and laughs of people, such dear, wonderful people, and all of a sudden Sylvia feels that push and gush of love, that thrill at the joy of life, the astonishment of being alive. Dopamine? Is that it? Whatever it is, it has eluded her for years, the orgasmic fleeting feeling of all being right with the world. Not since Daniel has she felt like this. It must be Devon, coming back here. It must be *right*. The sea is blue and bright and beautiful. How on earth can anybody recreate such a scene using paper and pencil? *The sea is surprisingly difficult to capture*, Geoffrey had said in the car. Sylvia had almost liked him then. How long, Sylvia contemplates as she finishes her Prosecco and gazes at the sky and the sea and the black cliffs, how long will it be until her daughter takes up pencil and sketchpad? She's an impressionable girl.

She takes in the blues and turquoises and greens, and the white edgings of the sea, the rustlings scrapings clickings hummings and swooshings of the pebbles caressed by the incessant waves. She regards the black of the cliffs over to the west of the bay. She was always wary of those cliffs, the way they loom out of the sea like pure fury, and she finds it almost impossible to contemplate them now. Once, she and a friend, in one of the hire boats, had rowed too close, and she remembers turning her back on them, looking towards the shore. They had overpowered her, and she could see from her friend's face that she wasn't alone in feeling frightened. She will not sail up close to them ever again, as some people are doing in these same little wooden rowing boats. The tiny boats, their tiny occupants, looking so vulnerable against the dark sheerness of the cliffs. They're better viewed from a distance. They're all right from there. She smokes. She puts on her sunglasses and her huge floppy sun hat. She is anonymous, which is her favourite state of being. She spots Geoffrey, further around the bay, facing the cliffs, and he appears to be sketching them, looking up, down, up, down, his pencil moving furiously across the sketch pad propped on his knees. He waves. About to wave back, she decides against it, and looks away from him, out to sea. Aren't artists supposed to be the most interesting of people?

Later, Sylvia wanders up to the shops, and buys a postcard. She finds a bench and after much deliberation, she writes her message on the card. She fishes around in her purse for a stamp, but she doesn't have one. She wanders along the street to the post office. Inside is cool and dark and empty. She has her pick of the windows, and makes for the old-ish woman in the middle.

'Where are you staying?' asks the lady as she carefully unpeels the requested single first class stamp.

'In a cottage at Rowan Park,' says Sylvia, and hands over the exact money. She may not have stamps, but she always tries to have change in her purse. The woman passes her the stamp under the screen.

'Have you seen him yet?'

31

'Who?'

'Old Theo.'

'He's around.'

'Queer story. Nobody knows if there's truth in it. But they swear it happened.'

'What happened?' Sylvia sticks her stamp to the card, and the woman offers to pop it in the sack, which is soon to be collected. Sylvia declines. She's heard it all before, of course. The stories and rumours. But it might be interesting to see if the rumours have intensified, as rumours are apt to do.

There was a woman, once, says the lady, who he loved, they say, but she betrayed him... nobody knows what happened. The lover, who was, she always understood, but she might be wrong, his brother, killed himself or Theo killed him, nobody *knows*, and ever since Old Theo has lived as a hermit and he's a broken man. Broken-hearted, you see. For love.

Sylvia blinks. It is so dark in here! And this odd tale again. One of those things, Sylvia suspects, that has grown over the years, grown out of all proportion, drifting further and further from the truth. Melodrama. Yet it doesn't sound at all unlikely. Theo always did have a *look* about him.

Sylvia thanks the woman, and steps back out into the sunshine. She sees Rosalie and Antonia across the street, emerging from one shop and heading into another. She doesn't call or wave, and they don't spot her. Sylvia notices that Antonia wears her plumpness well, like teenagers do. She looks supercool and, she supposes, rather hip, in black ragged skinny jeans and a Kurt Cobain T-shirt. She's into music now. Proper music. She loves that. They listen to CDs together in the car, and it has brought them a little closer, there's no doubt, this new-found

32

interest of Antonia's in the music of Sylvia's youth. But watching Antonia now, undetected, from this distance, Sylvia is worried. She barely recognises her daughter. And she doesn't need to diet! Is she being encouraged by Kelly-Marie? Sylvia has met her, once, and she seemed all right. Pretty, younger than Sylvia, of course, but not immature. Sylvia resolves to keep a close eye on her daughter this holiday. Perhaps she should talk to Anthony. Girls can be so... they can just be girls. Sylvia remembers it, the shying away from food, from chewing, from salivating, from swallowing, how easy it was to refuse.

But she's not convinced Anthony will listen to her concerns. He's the sort of man who insists on using the tumble dryer on even the warmest days.

She finds a postbox and examines her card. She runs her finger under the words. Has she spelled it all correctly? Too bad, if not. Is this wrong? What's it going to achieve? It's an act of desperation, isn't it? Pathetic, even. She sighs, and looks around, to be sure nobody is watching. Judging. But nobody is watching or judging. She posts it. Done now.

At the appointed time, she walks up to the tavern. Its garden is across a narrow road from the building, on a small promontory, delightful. Inside, the tavern is dark, and welcoming, and cool, like the post office. Geoffrey is at the bar already, with a near-empty glass. She approaches him, attempts to smile, and stands at the bar uncertainly, dithering over food, finally ordering for her and Antonia. Geoffrey has ordered for himself and Rosalie. Geoffrey offers to buy Sylvia a drink, and she accepts, not wanting to be churlish. She would like a Prosecco, thanks. Geoffrey says hang it, they'll have a bottle. Two. They emerge back out into the light, they cross the street, find

33

a table at the far end of the garden, and gaze out in silence at the dazzling blue sea.

'So fortunate with the weather, aren't we?' murmurs Geoffrey after the uncomfortable silence becomes unbearable. Small talk doesn't sit well with him, she guesses, and Sylvia doesn't like it much either, and it might be simpler to ask him to shut up. But it's so hot, and she decides not to be rude. He's being polite. She feels exhausted. Her postcard. *Did* she spell it right? Too late! Shit. What has she done?

'Great weather,' replies Sylvia. Silence, save the seagulls, the waves, the shouts of those people she felt she had loved an hour or so ago. People she doesn't know, and will never know, let alone love.

'I say, Sylvie, do you think we got off on the wrong foot?'

For a dreadful second, Sylvia thinks she may be sick.

'Don't you dare call me that,' she says. Spiteful, furious. She can feel herself aglow, red, tearful, trembling.

'I'm sor—'

'My name is Sylvia. It's Sylvi*a*. With an A.'

'Sorry. Right.'

He looks embarrassed, bewildered. It was an innocent remark, an unknowing choice of name. She must calm down. It was said in innocence, no matter how much of a prick he is. It's time to say something logical, she must switch off, forget about it. 'Something tells me you're not a Geoff,' she manages.

'Point taken.'

'Thank you.'

Oh, what a moment! To hear that name again.

*

In the first few seconds of their acquaintance, he was quiet and helpful. She found him confident, charming, intelligent. And he was all of those things, as she would later discover. It was the year eight parents' evening at Antonia's private school (Anthony paid, Anthony insisted). For some reason Anthony couldn't go to this parents' evening. So she was here alone, among all the parents who weren't her kind of people. Or she wasn't theirs. The evening was boring. Nobody wanted to be there. Antonia wanted her to speak to Mr Charpentier, her French teacher. Antonia was trying hard at French.

Mr Charpentier said, 'She tries.' His gaze was steady, so she gazed back. He cocked his head slightly to the left when delivering bad news. 'But she won't take the GCSE.'

'Don't want to anyway...'

'Antonia!'

'No matter. She can try Spanish. It's easier.'

'See? I'll try Spanish.'

Mr Charpentier laughed. And Sylvia felt something old drain out of her, and something new rush in, loud, gushing, unstoppable. She stopped her polite and fixed smiling. She no longer saw the French teacher, Mr Charpentier, she saw a man who intrigued her, and only afterwards, as they moved on to the next teacher, did she accept what had happened. She looked back and he smiled at her, and she knew, in that moment, her life had changed. His mannerisms were charming. He had the sweetest laugh.

Geoffrey looks askance at Sylvia. They are sitting at opposite corners of the table, neither of them in the shade of the parasol in the centre. Sylvia smokes.

35

'The others had better hurry up or lunch will be here before they are,' she says.

'Quite.'

'Antonia's going through a vegetarian stage.'

'Oh.'

'It's OK. It's her life. I want her to eat properly.'

'She's plumper than you are.'

Sylvia drags on her cigarette, and blows out the lungful slowly, towards the sea.

'You needn't smoke so much,' says Geoffrey, and takes a long gulp of his cider. He is leaving the Prosecco for her, it seems, but she can only have one more small glass. She has to drive back later.

'Needn't I?'

'No. It's not terribly attractive, to be perfectly honest, in women.'

'It's a good job I don't give a toss about what you do and don't find attractive then, isn't it? To be perfectly honest.'

'As you say.'

They both look out to sea.

'It was a mere observation,' he manages.

'You're a snob, Geoffrey,' says Sylvia, and she enjoys watching him squirm.

'So,' he says after another slug of cider, 'I take it we don't like each other? Well, you don't like me. I think you're rather smashing. But we don't want to create an atmosphere and ruin everybody's holiday, do we?'

'Darlings!'

And Rosalie, Antonia in tow, is here, announcing how she longs for a glass of that Prosecco.

Sylvia pats the bench and Antonia sits next to her.

'I've ordered a veggie burger for you,' says Sylvia. 'With chips and salad.'

'Thanks.'

'And here it is. Well-timed, you two,' says Sylvia, making an effort. A thin, eighteen-ish, self-conscious waiter carries towards them a tray laden with food. He glances at Antonia, and manages a half-smile, which she ignores. Geoffrey gallantly pours Prosecco for Rosalie. Sylvia puts her hand over her glass. 'No. Thank you.' Geoffrey pours a glass for Antonia, and passes it to her. She smiles and takes it. 'Just the one, Antonia,' Sylvia says.

Later, in the toilet, Antonia struggles with nausea, dizziness. Geoffrey had poured her another glass of Prosecco while Mum had wandered off on her own for a smoke. The toilets are not as nice as she'd expected, and the walls are a horrible orange, and have cracks in them, and there are dense, forgotten spider webs in the corners. The toilet roll dispenser is broken and a used sanitary pad sticks out from the lid of a small plastic bin. The toilet smells. The walls are damp.

Washing her hands, she studies herself in the mirror above the sink. She looks pink, but that can be put down to the weather. Her eyes seem to dance before her, skipping, skitting. She splashes water on to her face. She dries her face on her top; the towel hanging limply from its hook next to the hand basin is filthy. With a deep breath, she yanks open the Ladies' door, too hard, and it bangs into the wall ferociously. Luckily, the bar at the far end of the corridor is busy, and nobody notices, apart from Geoffrey, who waits for her in the corridor, foot against the wall, drinks held aloft on a tray.

'Don't worry, Antonia,' he says, staring at her. 'Cola this time. You've had enough.'

'I didn't ask—'

'Hush. It's fun, isn't it? So don't complain. That's your cola, and I got a coffee for your mother. Black and strong, as she seems to like it. Or should that be yours?'

Antonia reaches out and takes her drink, and he grins at her, white teeth gleaming, his blue-black hair shining even in the dim light of the corridor. YES says the tattoo. He follows her out to the garden. She walks deliberately, her knuckles white on the glass.

Antonia, tipsy, hot, spills the cola all over herself as she attempts to sit at the table.

'Shit!'

And Sylvia dabs at her with a handkerchief, earning for herself even more contempt from her daughter, and Rosalie also dabs at Antonia ineffectively, making a show of helping. The heat is getting to them all, Rosalie says. Should they go home?

At around half past one, with the sun high and hot, a different car arrives, black, sleek, and Theo watches as three occupants emerge, uncertain, stretching. Rosalie would normally be here to welcome the holiday-makers. She's done this job for years, taking care of the two holiday homes. All three of the cottages are still owned by the estate, of course, but managed by her. She is charged with meeting and greeting guests on arrival, and cleaning after they have gone home. She makes breakfast too. Often Theo smells the cooking, and it makes him salivate.

Perhaps it is demeaning work for her. She goes about it cheerfully enough. Presumably she is still paid. The current owners of Rowan Park seem like reasonable people. They haven't yet dispensed with her, or with him, for that matter. Possibly because the aura of eccentricity they generate between them adds a little elan to the estate? Something vaguely scandalous for locals and holidaymakers alike to speculate on? Who doesn't enjoy stories of local eccentrics? Who isn't thrilled by the sound of a dark rumour? Theo does not care. It is beyond and behind him now.

He watches as the new arrivals, hot and tired, debate what to do, after the taller man, dark-haired, has knocked on Rosalie's door and received no reply.

'Do you have a phone number?' the tall man says to the woman, who is petite and also black-haired. Theo doesn't like the way she stands, the way she moves, her pointed voice, pointed face, her elbows. She is all elbows. Full of herself. He doesn't like the look of the tall man, either. Even more full of himself.

'Yes, darling, of course,' pipes up the black-haired woman, shrill, 'but it's a landline, so absolutely no help if there's nobody in. She told me she lives next door... and would be here...'

'Shall we go for an amble?' says the other man, chunky, blond, a little pink-cheeked, not as good-looking as the other two, at least from a distance. The woman demurs about the milk, the bread, the bacon, eggs, orange juice. She reels off the list as though she were taking a school register. 'Shall we leave the cool box in the shade?'

The blond man takes the blue cool box from the back of the

car and puts it in the shade of the wall. He's a dogsbody. A gooseberry? The other two are a couple, obviously. Theo feels bad for him. He wants to warn him: be careful. Be cautious.

The taller man, in charge, locks up the car and they wander off. All three glance over towards Theo. He gazes back, almost raises his hand, but doesn't. No doubt they have been fore-warned about the hermit on the estate. Ignore him, Rosalie has probably said; he's a harmless fellow.

He sips tea and rolls up his trousers and luxuriates in the sun's heat on his bare legs, stretching himself out on the warm grass, like a cat. This is how a cat must feel, enjoying the mo-ment, enjoying the intense hard real sensation of heat, and not worrying about a thing.

Rosalie is apologetic. They got behind schedule in town, shop-ping, lunch, and such a beautiful day they all got so lazy and didn't want to move until Antonia spilled her drink and they had to return... Did they enjoy their walk? Lots to explore on the estate, they can ramble wherever they like, of course.

'Oh yes, thank you, we had a lovely walk, and the food in the ice box should have survived, not to worry if it hasn't, we'll eat it today anyway,' breathes the black-haired woman whose name is Caroline. Sylvia glances at the blond-haired man, who attempts a smile. She smiles back.

Antonia won't want neighbours. Especially a pretty woman with black hair and an amazingly prickly voice, and two boy-friends. *Weird*. The guests in the end cottage – Bluebell – have to walk through both of the other gardens to get to and from their door. Antonia won't like that either. It means if she sees them, or they see her, she'll have to be polite, and speak. It's rather an intrusion, and Sylvia recalls other holidaymakers tramping through the gardens, right past the windows, and some of them complaining, knocking on Rosalie's door and whining about the cottage, the lack of heat, the state of the furniture, demanding to know how the immersion heater worked.

When Antonia is in the bath, thank goodness, Geoffrey calls round with the promised bottles of Merlot. She thanks him and takes them. It's a genuine offer at neighbourliness, good will. It's also free wine, and a nice red at that.

'Rosalie says to ask you and Antoinette to pop round later for a drink with us. I think she's bored in the evenings.'

'Oh. All right. Antonia would like it. I'm tired.'

'Anto*nia*. Of course. My apologies. We'll see you later,' and he leaves, with, apparently, the grace to realise he's not welcome.

Theo closes his eyes, drowsy. The grass prickles his neck, and the earth is hot and hard beneath him. He has pulled his hat down over his face. He can't think properly if he's too hot, yet he loves to feel warm and cossetted, he welcomes the power of the heat. He loves the sun and the earth and lying on the earth, feeling it all moving over and through him. He recalls those bouncing blond curls, getting in her eyes, the extravagant swipe that made his heart beat faster. The swing of her hair. Laughing, laughing, a laughing girl.

She was thick with Theodore, any fool could see that. They had become Devon's answer to Cathy and Heathcliff, Helena had

41

often thought, but not too seriously, until now. Their... close friendship... was noticeable, too noticeable, and perturbing. Helena was not going to entertain any nonsense and neither was Simon, and so she decided to have a word with her middle son, now her eldest son. How difficult it was to grow used to that. She never would. Meredith would always be, in her heart, her oldest, most-loved son. Theodore and Clement had their place, of course. But they were in second place, and third place.

She was surprised to discover how determined Theodore was. He'd always been quietly headstrong. He was nineteen years of age, stubborn like his father, and handsome (and stubborn) like dear Meredith. How alike they were. She couldn't tell if that brought comfort or sorrow. She spoke to Theodore of her... concerns...

So he asked his mother not to worry, which was his way of telling her to keep her nose out of his affairs.

'Is this a love affair? You're too young.' Haughty. *Young* was a euphemism. Lazy. Transparent. She tilted her head back as she always did when she was curious, when she was cross, when she was aroused by any sort of feeling. She knew she had this tic and she corrected it while waiting for Theo's reply.

'I don't know what it is,' said Theo.

And it was true. He didn't know. He didn't truly know what a "love affair" was. But he supposed he was having one.

'Do you love her?' his mother continued.

'Yes.'

'But as a sister? Yes? Theodore?'

He lowered his head. 'Not as a sister.'

'You do know it is out of the question.'

'I... I don't know. I hadn't thought of it. But I don't agree with you, Mother.'

'Then you shall hear it from your father.'

'I shall hear it from nobody.'

For four years he and Rosalie had been physically close. They had learned things together. Lots of things. They were inseparable.

Later, his father was blunt. 'Theodore, you fool, you cannot... *marry* her,' he said. He must not, in any circumstances, have relations with her. There must not be a child, categorically. Did he understand? Her people were good people, hardworking, loyal, and he had no wish to offend them. Her father liked to take a drink, of course; and he could see in their daughter a certain looseness of morals, slackness in her behaviour. She was *that-sort-of-girl,* he said, and Theo winced. But there may be truth in it. They had been together many times. Tumbling, intense, daring encounters that had left both of them breathless, dazed. But this he kept to himself, and always would. He knew they knew, or thought they knew, his mother and father, they must have realised it, or there would be no need for this "discussion".

They were careful together. He had a number of ways of avoiding pregnancy, and so did she. Tricks. Methods. They were not stupid, far from it. They did other things, at other times. Theo knew he was blessed, favoured, to be having such experiences at such a young age with a girl like her. She was seventeen now, and she was enthusiastic and she was willing. Nobody knew their secret, even though it wasn't a secret. It was simply that neither of them had ever told anybody about it. They had never felt the need to.

'What on earth do you think your brother would counsel you to do?' asked Father. Theo hated it when his parents invoked Meredith's name, his authority, each time they wanted to speak to him of something "important". Meredith was dead, and Theo was pretty certain Meredith had died without direct knowledge of the female body. That was part of his brother's tragedy. So Theo felt he knew exactly what his much-missed Meredith would counsel; but he said nothing of this to his father.

Hell, he was nineteen, he could do as he chose. It was his life, and if this girl handed herself to him as she did, he was not going to turn her away. Besides, he loved her. He *loved* her. He loved her more than anybody he had ever met or known, apart from Meredith. He was wise enough already to know when to separate lust from love. For her he felt both, but never at the same time.

'It's high time you got a proper job. A decent life. Get yourself off to university, boy. I can pull a few strings. Good god, you have a brain and you shall go!'

Theo stood silent and insolent, waiting to be dismissed, aware of his father's deep sigh, the impatient squeak of the brandy decanter, and his mother's equally deep sigh, and her taffeta dress, the black one with the white polka dots, rustling like the hydrangea bushes that grew either side of the drawing room windows, ruffled in the soft September breeze.

Sylvia cleans the inside of her car; Antonia has the unfortunate habit of throwing sweet wrappers and drink cartons on to the floor, despite Sylvia's frequent requests for her not to do so. After a long journey the car tends to be swamped in debris.

44

It's dusty too, so she wipes the dashboard with baby wipes that she always keeps in her glove compartment. The car smells of cigarettes, but she doesn't mind that.

Sylvia smokes too much, and watches too much TV, and there is something lacking in her life; not only Antonia, and not only Daniel. But what? Sylvia wishes she could feel differently, pull herself together. She always ends up back here in her mind, castigating herself. She supposes the worst thing about her is the smoking. That's what she can comfortably tell herself. But it isn't the worst thing. Carefully she wipes the steering wheel.

It saddens and pleases her that Antonia has grown out of all things pink; Barbie dolls and baby dolls she once held so dear. Fairies and princesses. All gone, all forgotten, replaced by Converse shoes, skinny jeans, tight-fitting black tops, skimpy underwear, and heavy black liquid eye-liner. And boy talk. Lots of boy talk. At least, Sylvia says to herself, at least Antonia does talk to her about such things, sometimes. Yet she fears she may talk to Kelly-Marie too. More. How jealous that makes her feel. Desperate. Sylvia barely recognises this young woman who has replaced her daughter. Sometimes she is convinced that the young Antonia – squeaky voice, pigtails, and tantrums – is still in there, hiding, and will burst out soon and say *Hello–did–you–miss–me?* It's hard to accept she has gone, and gone forever. And now the two of them are in transition, getting to know each other all over again, like when Antonia was born, and Sylvia became a mother, trying to breastfeed, trying to change a nappy confidently. It took time then, it will take time now, this rebirth, this new incarnation of Antonia. Yet Sylvia is uncertain they even like each other. She loves her daughter, of

45

course, for what she is, her daughter. But their estrangement is obvious; Antonia spends more time at her father's house than hers, and it's heart-breaking, but what can she do? Antonia is almost sixteen, a young woman becoming free to make her own decisions. Yet Antonia chose to live with her father several years ago, and Sylvia knows why, and she deserves it. No. The smoking habit is not the worst thing about her.

'Nice poem,' says Geoffrey. 'Who are you reading?'

'Plath, of course,' says Rosalie.

'Of course.'

'I've been a fan for many years. I should have grown out of her, but I can't shake her off.'

Geoffrey beams disingenuously at Sylvia. 'Are you a poetry buff too?' he asks.

'I don't really understand poetry,' says Sylvia. 'Although I love Mary Oliver.'

Daniel had brought (bought?) her a present, once, wrapped in grey tissue paper, tied with a green ribbon. It was a copy of Mary Oliver's *Why I Wake Early*. She and Daniel are (*were*) both early risers.

'Oh, I don't read women poets,' says Geoffrey. 'Incomprehensible twaddle. Even Plath. Mind you, so is men's poetry. Apart from Betjeman. I don't think the poets understand it themselves, do you? If the truth be told?'

'Probably not,' says Sylvia.

'Oh, I won't have that!' says Rosalie, closing her book.

'Can I top up your wine?' says Geoffrey to Sylvia, brandishing the bottle.

'Yes, please.' She reaches across for a refill. She won't look at him. But for Antonia she wouldn't be here.

'Rosalie? Another? It's good.' Geoffrey passes back Sylvia's glass, smiling broadly at her.

'Why not? Your father always did have good taste in wines.'

'And stacks of dosh to buy them with. By the way, did you get his cheque? He said he'd send it this week.' Geoffrey takes Rosalie's glass from her, carefully fills it, and hands it back with a friendly grin.

'Of course. I paid it into the bank this morning. Your father is always punctilious about such things.'

Geoffrey puts the empty bottle on to the floor. 'Unlike me. I'm hopeless with money. Shall I open another?' He grins at Antonia. She is sipping at a glass, but it's obvious to all that she doesn't like it.

'An artist should be hopeless with money,' says Rosalie. She takes another sip. 'This *is* good. Let's drink all the wine! It's the holidays.'

'Excuse me. I'm going for a smoke,' says Sylvia, rising from the sofa, clutching her handbag and her full glass of wine. She feels them all looking at her as she leaves the room. She senses the grimaces, the shrugs. She doesn't care.

Theo brews tea. The night has settled on the world and it's his time, his time to listen and think. All that remembering, which he doesn't do, but of course does. It can't be good for him. But he has promises to keep and he will keep them, as he always has. The promises are all he has now; and Rosalie, her presence, her home, beyond the hedge, only yards from him. Yet the gulf between them is immense, and it has always been immense, despite the early years, that intensity. They were play-

47

ing games; *she* was playing games. He'd thought it real. But for Rosalie, nothing is ever real.

The reappearance of Sylvia, after all these years, is worrying. Does she know? Anything? If she knew, would she be here? He shivers. She shouldn't have come. She shouldn't have brought her daughter. This is no place for a daughter.

TUESDAY

Geoffrey eats Rosalie's eggs and bacon with his wolfish relish, but he does not eat greedily, Sylvia has to admit. He has manners in that regard. He's something of an enigma. Hateful, but affable. Ugly, but handsome. And his paintings: unremarkable, but striking. Sylvia had glimpsed his work in the studio after cleaning her car yesterday. The door to the rustic-style studio was open, but Geoffrey was not around. His work was oddly lifeless, and drab, but somehow substantial. His paintings appeared to be mostly portraiture; but a couple of still lifes too, she thought. It was hard to tell.

Antonia again manages to join them for breakfast, and nibbles at toast, sips her orange juice.

'Antonia,' says Sylvia, 'shall we do something today?'

'Like what?'

'Shopping?'

'Where?'

'Let's go to Exeter.'

'I don't want to go to Exeter.'

'Let's do something else then.'

'Like what?'

Antonia smiles broadly at Geoffrey as he finishes his breakfast. Sylvia realises she is beaten.

'Now then,' says Rosalie, leaning across the table towards Antonia and taking her hand, 'why don't you help me today?'

And so it is arranged. Antonia is to spend the morning with Rosalie, doing god knows what, and Geoffrey is going out sketching.

Sylvia volunteers to wash Rosalie's dishes; it feels like the right thing to do, as Rosalie works hard making breakfast. Sylvia enjoys washing the dishes in the cool, silent kitchen, after the others have dispersed; she can hear Antonia somewhere upstairs giggling with Rosalie, as they make beds. It's a simple and homely pleasure to be domestic in somebody else's house. Sylvia sweeps the kitchen floor. Then she smokes a cigarette sitting out on Rosalie's terrace. Another beautiful day, the world hushed and silenced in the valley, with only the residual hum of insects and bees. It must be too hot already for the donkeys to summon up the energy to make their strange, comforting braying noises, but Sylvia can see them dotted about in their field on the other side of the valley: little plastic farmyard figures thoughtfully arranged by a lonely child. Woodsmoke curls up from Theo's fire, where he is boiling his kettle for tea. If she were to go closer, speak to him... would he invite her to join him? She might like to... there are questions she would like to ask. Would he bark at her, as he used to bark at the guests? 'Be off!'

Theo dressed himself, and helped Rosalie to get dressed too.

'My parents want me to break it off,' said Theo, simply. There was no point in being coy. Rosalie was seldom coy.

She pulled on one of her stockings while he did the other for her. He kissed her thigh.

'They know?' she said.

'They suspect, at least. They say I can't marry you.'

'Were you intending to marry me?'

'I don't think so. I hadn't thought about it until they mentioned it.'

'I see. I'm never getting married. So there's no problem there, dear Theo.'

Rosalie pulled on her frock, she fiddled with her hair. He left off helping, and watched her. She studied herself in the large mirror over the fireplace. The drawing room was one of their favoured venues. There was something so open about it, and the risk of being discovered was immense, which appealed to them both; but it had never yet happened. The hydrangeas, rattling around outside in the breeze, tap-tap-tapping on the French windows, were the only observers.

'Wouldn't you marry me if I asked?' he said, aghast at her flippancy.

She ruffled up her fair curls, combed through them with her thin fingers. 'Good god, no. So don't ever ask, Theo, please. Everything is fine as it is. We have fun, don't we? Let's enjoy this while we can.'

'Is it only fun? For you, I mean?' Theo finished dressing himself, pulling on his shoes.

'Yes.'

'Do you have others?'

'Other men?'

'Yes. That's what I mean. Other men.'

Rosalie turned from the mirror to face him. 'Yes. But not

since you and I...'

'But you were fourteen!'

'Thirteen. So?'

'How many?'

'Some.'

And of course he was disappointed, and surprised, and later that night, alone in bed, he thought hard about his "carrying on" with Rosalie, and about what his parents had said, and he wondered if they might be right. He cared more for her than she did for him, obviously. But she was... she was a lover he could not give up. Together they were magical and twisted, and he could not let that slip away from him in the name of propriety. She was his mistress, he felt, he knew, and he saw no reason why she couldn't always be that. If he were to ask her if their arrangement could remain in place, for ever, indefinitely, no matter what, no matter who else, he felt sure she would say, *Yes. Of course. Why do you even ask?*

Daniel allowed Sylvia to be herself, and they spoke, a lot, about her life. Nobody else had ever shown real interest in her life. Sylvia was bored in her job... she'd like to work at the local cinema again. Daniel laughed, and she explained how much she loved films, she escaped into them, she loved to watch them over and over again, even the shit ones, and it wasn't that funny. He stopped chuckling and rubbed her shoulder, stroked her cheek.

Daniel had been married for eleven years, but there were no children. He wanted to be a father. His wife was not "ready" to be a mother. She was forty-six years old, Daniel told Sylvia. Sylvia said nothing. She didn't know the woman. She was sleeping with her husband. There was nothing she could say.

Sylvia tries not to think about Daniel these days. Their affair has taken on much too big a significance in her memory: it was perfect, it seems to her now, when surely it wasn't. It was divine and pure and righteous, in her memory. Daniel has become for her a mythical hero. But he was a disaster; and their affair, and its fallout, has shaped the pattern of her life since those heady days, those days of rain and hotel rooms and secrecy, and eventually, ruin. She won't ever forgive herself, or him, but she still misses him. She misses herself *with* him. With him she knew she had been the best version, the most colourful and fun version, of herself. She smiled with him, laughed with him, flirted with him, mercilessly, always.

Sylvia wanders down to the hedge, where there is a small gap that opens out into the field. The hermitage is quiet; the fire waning; the door is open, presumably to air out the hut. It must get hot at this time of year, on days like these. She suspects Theo is not there. Sylvia approaches slowly, feeling like a trespasser. She peers into the dark interior, murmurs a tentative 'Hello?' and waits for a reply. There is no reply, and she enters the hermitage, she stands on its threshold. It is surprisingly clean and tidy. The bed is made up with a thick eiderdown, which Sylvia recognises. Was it not on her bed in Rose all those years ago? It looks sheeny and old and colourless, but she's certain it's the same one. A bookshelf, stacked with books. A cupboard in the corner. A beaten old chest of drawers is bare save for an old jam jar sitting on top, containing a single rhododendron spray; an oddly feminine touch. Next to the bed is a small rug, and a three-legged stool, on which sits a candle and a box of matches. It all looks glorious and Sylvia feels a pang of – what? Jealousy? Envy. For the simple life, unadorned and untroubled.

Theo's life is not untroubled, of course; that is the point. He's not "all there", he is scarred emotionally, anybody can guess at that, and Sylvia is pretty sure who he is scarred by. She remembers the lady in the post office, her talk of the rumours. Sylvia is curious. Yet, he is a frightening man, prone to temper. She *heard*. She has warned Antonia not to go near him, not to bother him. He's a private individual, and unpredictable. Best left alone.

He must have gone for a walk, or he's performing his ablutions in the stream in the woods. She backs out of the hermitage, with reluctance, and looks around, but there is no sign of him.

One of the guests who arrived yesterday is in the garden at Bluebell. Is he smoking? She loves the company of other nicotine addicts. It's a camaraderie she craves, with the numbers dwindling year on year. Nothing makes her feel more validated than another smoker. She slowly returns to Rosalie's garden. Yes, the man is definitely smoking. She can smell it. She'll catch Theo another time, if she dares. Her courage is as absent as Theo, evaporated into the sun-filled air. Before she knows it—

'Morning!' she calls over, bright, fake.

'Oh, hi. Hello. I'm sneaking a cheeky smoke. Hope you don't mind.'

'God, no, I'm about to do the same. Can I get a light? I used my last match.'

Not true, of course. He's a nice-looking man. As in, nice person. Vaguely handsome underneath the pounds. Blond hair, thick, neatly cut. About her height.

'Come and join me on the bench?' she says, and he smiles, and hurries over. He offers her a cigarette, and lights it for her, his hand pink and trembling. They sit alongside each other, looking across the field.

'I'm Sylvia,' she says, between drags. She offers her hand, and he takes it, in a firm but trembling grip, and they shake.

'I'm Chris.'

A companionable silence blossoms among the plumes.

'You're on holiday with... your... friends?'

'You've noticed.'

'I'm not sure what I've noticed, but yes, I've noticed.'

'I'm a doormat, Sylvia.'

'How so?' She takes a drag, scrutinising his pink face. He needs a bit of sun, a bit of exercise. A black T-shirt?

'I live with my girlfriend and her latest fancy man. We live together. Three of us. Actually I think Tom is her boyfriend now. I don't know what I am.'

A tiny cough, a deep drag, a think. How do you react to that? And is he trying not to *cry*? Oh god, say something!— 'Yes, sounds like you are a doormat.'

An awkward look, an uncertainty, then a smile, a laugh. 'You're right, Sylvia. You're absolutely right.'

'Why do you put up with it?'

'I've nowhere else to go. That's the truth. I don't even have a job at the moment. Caroline... she's an open house person. Without her I'd be out on the street. I've nothing.'

'So you stay and put up with nonsense.'

'Yes.'

They drag on their cigarettes.

In the distance, Theo emerges from the trees at the bottom of the field. Too late. She'll try another time. She knows what she wants to ask Chris, of course.

'Have you ever...?'

'What?'

'That.'

'Oh. Yes.'

'Blimey.'

'Not recently. I'm relegated to one of the spare rooms.'

'Thank goodness.'

They drag on their cigarettes.

'It made me feel sick.'

'I'm sorry. You should leave. Is there nowhere you could go?'

'My sister would put me up. Probably. If I asked her. She kicked her husband out not long ago. She's got bigger balls than I have.'

Sylvia shrugs. Theo approaches his hut. He's carrying a towel, a sponge bag. He could almost be returning from a campsite shower block.

Chris nods towards Theo. 'What's his story?'

'That I don't know. I never asked. He was part of the furniture.'

'I thought you are on holiday here?'

'I am. Sort of. I was brought up here. Rosalie Rawe is my mother. *Estranged* mother. My daughter wanted to meet her. So I decided to come back. We're here for a fortnight.'

'Blimey. My turn to say that.'

'Blimey indeed. It's tough being around her again. I wanted Antonia – my daughter – to see where I grew up. But it was a

56

mistake.'

Chris shrugs. 'Life *is* mistakes, isn't it?'

'Yes, I suppose so. What do you do for a living when you're working?'

'Anything. I've no career. I've worked in supermarkets, factories, been a cab driver, you name it. I don't know what I want to be when I grow up.'

'Not many of us do!'

'So I drift about in this one life I will ever have and basically act like a stupid fucker.'

'No, you're all right. I think the stupid fuckers are those other two.'

'Thanks.'

'And you need to get out of it. Now.'

'Today?'

'Ideally.'

She doesn't know what to say. Funny how strangers offload sometimes, and allow you to poke at their weaknesses, to peer in, creating a queer sort of illumination in the dark. A Caravaggio moment. They finish their cigarettes.

'If it's making you unhappy you should bite the bullet. Move out. Rent. I had to. It's fine.'

'How much do you pay?'

'Six-nine-five a month. Not too bad. Two-bedroomed flat. Antonia, my daughter, she only stays sometimes. She lives with her dad.'

And it's weird to say this for the first time, but it's out. Up for discussion. 'Actually I persuaded her to come on holiday with me. I hoped we might reconnect. But we won't.'

'There's not much here for a teenage girl to do...'

'Do you have kids?'

'No. Never wanted children, but maybe that was wrong too. I don't know myself much.'

'None of us do, Chris.'

'So did you leave home when you were young?'

'I was seventeen. Never came back, until now.'

'Why? Why to both of those.'

'She... Rosalie... was... she is... a complete and utter bitch. Selfish, unaware, a dangerous person.'

'So why come back?'

'To be a daughter again. So I can understand Antonia. I've let her down.'

She has never said this even to herself, in her heart. She hadn't known this, until now. But of course. This is why she is here. To be a daughter again.

'You're not a bad mother though.'

Drag. Silence. Hold. Release. Theo, back at his hut, alone, sitting on his log, preparing tea. He can't hear, she's certain, he's too old, too far away.

'Yes, Chris, I am. I'm a terrible mother.'

Had she known Theo wasn't there, kidding herself all along? She could be stupid like that sometimes. Dancing around things, pretending to herself that she's thinking one way, while acting another. It's what happens. She would like to talk to him. She never has. It was frowned upon, discouraged, by Rosalie. *Leave poor Theo alone. He doesn't want to talk to anybody. He bites.*

Sylvia knows he doesn't bite. He's not crazy. Far from it. Crazed. There's that look about him, not of fear; a silent rampage behind the blue eyes. She suspects his memories are thick

58

and clodding, impossible to shake off. And she will talk to him. She really will.

Chris obliterates his cigarette stub and stands up. 'Thanks for the talk. You're straight. Straight-talking.'

Sylvia smiles, and stamps out her own cigarette. 'Is there any point in being anything else? Say what you mean, and mean what you say.'

'Are you in love?'

'What?'

'Are you in love.'

A week after the parents evening, Daniel Charpentier rang her. Totally unexpected, unprofessional too. He wanted to take her to dinner. She heard herself agreeing to this. A date made. Difficult to arrange. She organised a sleepover for Antonia; she made sure it was a weekend when Anthony would be away.

Daniel was on the verge of separation. He was tired of no babies, tired of the disappointment. They had grown apart. Had stopped having sex. Had stopped talking.

She liked the way he poured wine. They had chosen a red, and they drank two bottles between them. She could barely eat and the air between them sucked them both in, suffocating.

And the second date, an agonising month later, he came to her home, the home she shared with Anthony and Antonia, dismissed like ghosts who weren't believed in as she kissed Daniel in the hallway, the dinner she had prepared, barely touched, the wine consumed rapidly. She wasn't nervous. And when they made it to her bed, and later the bath, she counted herself lucky. She felt herself living, after years of being dead.

*

Chris is waiting. Says something.

'Sorry, what?' she says. 'I was miles away.'

'I said, never mind the love question, that was me being a nosy git. And I said I bet you're not a bad mum.'

'How much do you want to bet?'

Antonia and Rosalie are preparing lunch in Rose cottage. Sylvia decides not to join them. They won't miss her. She goes up to her room in Columbine and lowers herself stiffly on to the bed. Her joints have been stiffening slowly for years, of course. For some time she has been less able to leap up off the floor with the alacrity of youth. She's not old at fifty-one. But neither is she young. Not that she would like to be young again. The menopause is a drag, but at least she's done with menstruation. Such a release. Now she lives a little more like how men live. She likes it. Hot flushes aside.

She's tired. Oh, so tired. Long ago she made up her mind she doesn't – can't – will never – love her mother. That's a heart-breaking thing. But it isn't possible to love Rosalie. And now, history repeating itself, her own daughter doesn't love *her*. And it's too much to bear, and Sylvia bursts into lonely tears. *Straight-talking. Are you in love.* She cries alone whenever she cries. She won't burden her workmates at the cinema. She won't burden her neighbour. She won't burden her friends, the two women she regards as friends, but whom she rarely sees. When she does see them, there is no room for tears. Daniel is gone and Anthony is gone and now too Antonia is gone and that is of course the root of the tears which will continue to

60

flow even when there should be no more tears. Yet there are always more tears.

It wasn't Antonia's fault, any of it.

What is Daniel doing now? She can't help but wonder. Teaching in a new school? No longer teaching? She hopes he is thinking of her. She can't believe he isn't. Can't bear the thought that he isn't. His address on the electoral roll showed two names. His name and a woman's name. But so what? So what. *You say what you mean. Straight-talking.*

'Mum!'

'What? Yes?' She must have dropped off to sleep. She sits up, smoothes her hair.

Antonia bursts into the bedroom. 'I'm going sketching with Geoffrey.'

'You're what?'

'I'm going sketching with Geoffrey.'

'Sketching?'

'Yeah. Wake up! Mum, he's being nice. He wants to teach me to draw. What's wrong with that?'

'Nothing. Where are you going?'

Antonia is thumping back down the stairs. 'To the meadow, he said. Bye!'

'Wait! Have you had lunch?'

But Antonia has gone.

Sylvia gets up.

Sylvia, silent, barely daring to breathe, two yards away, behind the thick hedge. She can't see much. The top of Geoffrey's head, his sleek black hair. *Sketching? Yeah.* Poor Antonia. She's no country girl. She's an alien there, in that sweet meadow, the hot Devon sun pouring down on her, the flowers motionless, poised, waiting to be drawn. Sylvia breathes slowly, calmly, straining to listen. There's a gate a few yards away and if things— if she is needed, she will saunter through it, casually, innocently, and wander over to them. And ask to see their drawings.

It sounds as though Antonia is sitting alongside Geoffrey. Their quiet voices are close together. Is she drawing? Can't tell. Possibly she can't draw at all, or feels she can't. Sylvia remembers feeling like that as a youth, that crippling lack of self-belief. Older than youth. Still here. Always here. Not good enough for Daniel. She wasn't. He was quick to disappear as soon as the shit hit the fan. She might have hoped for more. Fears he is a coward. Or is she a coward? They both are, probably. She'd hoped he might have stuck around, stayed with her. They could have braved it out together. No need for shame.

'What's that flower?' asks Antonia.

'That is a foxglove.'

'Foxglove,' says Antonia thoughtfully. Had she not heard the name before? It was possible. Kids these days... words missing in dictionaries... *foxglove.*

'I believe it comes from folks glove. Folks, as in little folk. Fairies. That sort of thing.'

'There is no such thing as fairies,' says Antonia, babyishly. Her age... fifteen. Two days shy of her sixteenth birthday. At once a child and a woman. Dangerous.

'So what?' says Geoffrey.

'What's the name of the flower you're sketching?'

'This is a columbine.'

'Oh.'

'Pretty little flower, isn't it?'

'It's all right.'

Geoffrey, with a sigh, puts down his sketchpad. Sylvia parts leaves, green growth, the smell of earth , dampness, animal, an animal smell, like at the cottages. She leans forward. Teeters on the edge of balance. Thorns and brambles waiting for her. She watches, listens, as Geoffrey reaches out and touches a strand of Antonia's blond hair.

'I think you are the prettiest flower in the whole meadow,' he says. Then he laughs.

He crouches behind her, and teaches her how to hold the pencil. She holds it clumsily, but she tries. She wants to please him, Sylvia can tell.

'The secret is,' he says, taking up his own sketchpad again, 'that you must try to forget this is a columbine, forget this is a flower at all. Simply try to recreate what you see, with your eyes, not with your knowledge. Do you understand?'

She nods slowly. She stares at the flower and starts to draw it.

If that man...! But she needs to chill out, as Antonia might say. If she could see a little more...

There is no sign of anybody else, anywhere. The valley is swamped in the heat of the afternoon, but teeming with quiet life, grasshoppers chirping, bees pottering among the poppies, sky larks above, angels' voices, soaring unseen over the earth. Antonia and Geoffrey are silent. Sylvia leans even further forward, a nettle stings her arm, and with fortitude she ignores it. Is Geoffrey kissing Antonia? What the—?! Slowly, sweating, why now, oh god, why a hot flush *now*? – she steps back from

63

the hedge, disentangling herself, takes another backward step. Then she walks, slowly, stealthily, towards the gate. Wipes sweat from her face, her neck.

'What's that flower called?' says Antonia, pointing.

'That is a foxglove,' says Geoffrey.

She's out of place here. Should she know the names of these flowers? Does he think her ignorant?

Geoffrey is sketching. Antonia is sitting alongside him, watching. He's provided her with a sketchpad and told her to give it a go. So far she hasn't attempted anything. She can't draw.

'Foxglove,' says Antonia. Has she heard the name before? Must have!

'I believe it comes from folks glove. Folks, as in little folk. Fairies. That sort of thing.'

'There is no such thing as fairies,' says Antonia.

'So what?'

She has no reply, so she sits and looks around her, sighing. 'What's the name of the flower you're sketching?'

'This is a columbine.'

'Oh.'

'Pretty little flower, isn't it?'

Antonia shrugs. 'It's all right.'

Geoffrey, with a sigh, puts down his sketchpad. He reaches out and touches a strand of her blond hair. 'I think you are the prettiest flower in the whole meadow,' he says. She blushes furiously, whips her hair away from him, and takes up her sketchpad. He laughs. Did he really say that? Did he mean it?

He crouches behind her and teaches her how to hold the

pencil. She holds it clumsily, but she tries. She wants to please him. 'The secret is,' he says, taking up his own sketchpad again, 'you must try to forget this is a columbine, forget this is a flower at all. Simply try to recreate what you see, with your eyes, not with your knowledge. Do you understand?'

She nods slowly, not speaking. She already doesn't know what it is. But she doesn't need to unlearn, only learn. She stares at the flower and starts to draw it.

'There you are!'

They spring apart. Antonia red-faced. Geoffrey not.

'I've come to see your work,' Sylvia says, putting on her best disinterested voice. 'Show me.'

Antonia stares at her in disbelief, disgust. She hands the sketchpad to Geoffrey, stands, and marches towards the gate.

'Well?' says Sylvia.

'What?'

'I don't recall Antonia asking me if she could go off with you.'

'I don't think she did ask you.'

'She *told* me.'

'Actually, she asked Rosalie.'

Sylvia pulls herself up as tall as she can manage, tall, matching Geoffrey. 'What has Rosalie got to do with anything?'

'I expect Antonia thought in lieu of you, Rosalie would do.'

'No. She won't do.'

'Rosalie's pretty cool about most things. It might be good for Antonia to learn to sketch. That was all.'

'What are you, some kind of paedophile?'

Geoffrey looks taken aback. Then horrified. She does not know where the question came from. She doesn't trust him. But she can't accuse him. Antonia must have kissed boys at school. But Geoffrey is not a boy, he's a grown man, and he is vile. But accusing him of *that*... she's not going to apologise. Not yet. Were they even kissing? Did she imagine it? Possibly. Possibly not.

Geoffrey sighs. 'No.'

'Good. How old are you?'

'I'm thirty-eight.'

'A little old for a not-quite-sixteen-year-old then? Over twice her age.'

'It was a sketching expedition. I'm sorry. It was wrong of me.'

'Yes, it was.'

'It's not like I'm a teacher,' he says, and the wolf grin is back, leering. So Antonia must have told him.

'Oh, fuck off.'

This is Rosalie's fault. How could she... How *dare* she give "permission"? It's not her place, not at all.

They shouldn't have come. It was always going to be a disaster. She should have told Antonia the truth. The reason for Sylvia leaving home at seventeen, never to return, until now, all these years later. Humiliation is a hard emotion to deal with, and it's better not spoken of. Especially between mothers and daughters, where mothers must not admit, ever, to humiliation. It weakens a mother. It makes her daughter turn from her in disgust. And it has happened once, and Sylvia is hellbent on ensuring it doesn't happen again. So she is back at the

66

cottages, back in the valley, back in the company of her mother who has never apologised, as far as Sylvia knows, for anything.

Thank god. This day is done. Antonia, laid out on the rug. Bored. Ignoring Sylvia as much as she can.

'Why don't you read?'

'You know I don't like reading.'

'Can we talk?'

About what? Sylvia knows this is what Antonia is thinking. *No, we can't.* Of course. *We have nothing to talk about.*

'Who is that woman next door?'

'I don't know, darling, somebody else on holiday.'

'Why does she have two boyfriends?'

'She doesn't. The blond-haired man, he's their friend. He's nice.'

'I don't like her. She wants to jump Geoffrey.'

'Antonia!'

'She does! She's a tart.'

Sylvia sighs, and she can see it's no good trying to talk to Antonia tonight. They are approaching dangerous ground.

'Dad called you a tart once.'

Trying to hurt her now. She can handle this. 'I'm sure he did.'

'He was drunk. Kelly-Marie told him to be quiet.'

'That was good of her.'

'It's because I was there.'

They say nothing for a while. Then: 'I'm going for a bath.'

'I wasn't spying on you earlier. I wanted to make sure you were OK. And I wanted to see your sketches.'

'Yeah, right. Mum, I don't believe you.'

67

'Don't go near that man again. He's not a good person.'

'And you are?'

And she's gone, for her bath, and the water runs overhead, thumping into the tub, and Sylvia is alone once more.

WEDNESDAY

It was Antonia's idea, wasn't it, to come here? She wanted to meet her grandmother. *Why had she never seen her?* Anthony had – probably out of spite – last summer told Antonia all he knew about the grandmother neither he nor Antonia had ever met. Antonia asked questions: why? why? why? Sylvia had tried to answer but later, a year later, she suggested to Antonia they go to Devon, and meet her grandmother. Antonia agreed. She was curious, and cross, because she had always wanted a "Nanna". Anthony's mother was long dead.

So that's why they are here. Yes. That's what she's telling herself, and everybody else. Apart from Chris. He has the gift of getting the truth out of her. Antonia seems to love Rosalie, as Sylvia had known she would. Rosalie and her welcoming arms, the ability to draw people in, and the ability to push them away, as she always does, in the end. Any woman who can push her own daughter away can push anybody.

They are here now. May as well stick it out. Sylvia rolls over, faces the window through which sunlight pours. It's warm on her face. She checks her phone: it's 5:53. She'll get up... in a minute...

A movement, an energy, a life event, her biggest, an end to the stillness that had hidden her away for too long. Whatever it was, it was real, she had it, and now it's gone. It can't be retrieved.

'Sylvie,' she whispers into the bright quiet bedroom. 'I'll call you Sylvie.'

There were other women, she found out later, not only his wife. Other *women*. He didn't seem to understand how that hurt her feelings. He had no conscience when it came to women, and sex, and love. Oh, he had never loved her! Tricks. To get her to sleep with him. In other ways he did have a conscience. She couldn't figure him out, couldn't see his point of view. His flippancy...

Once, they'd had that glorious bath together. His idea. He read poems to her. French poems she could not understand, but it was enough to be read to, his effortless French accent blending with the words, the hot water, the lavender. It was a night like no other, a night she had always wanted but felt she would never have, but she had it, and she would remember it, and nobody, not even Daniel, could ever take it from her. The romance. The memory. It was hers. She'd been innocent then, about the other women. The word. The lowly word. *Womaniser*.

It refuses to drain away in the shower. She tries to wash it away, this longing, taking her again in its ugly ruthless grip. It's the longing she can't stand. Almost she wishes she had never met Daniel. That night, their best night, that single night she had felt loved like she had never felt loved before, or since.

Memories are cruel. Impressions, crueller. Both, often, wrong.

She steps out, dries herself, puts on a frock and sandals. She stops by Antonia's room, and listens. Nothing. Door closed.

She'll have a coffee and a cigarette. Later she'll have breakfast with Rosalie and Geoffrey. Today she is hungry. Today she will eat.

Geoffrey asks half a dozen eager questions about the "amazing woman" in the other cottage. What's the deal? A threesome? You're joking? Bloody hell. He's an open-minded kind of man but *really*?

Rosalie looks blank, unsinterested. Not shocked. Sylvia can't recall her mother ever looking shocked. She makes breakfast, serves breakfast, acts like Sylvia is any other guest, and probably that is for the best. It can't be any other way now, too much separation, estrangement, the gap too wide to be bridged. She doesn't want to bridge it anyway. She's just another holidaymaker.

And outside, down at the hut, Theo is waking up too. A hot day in the valley is nigh, and he will rise, eat fruit, drink tea, wash, snooze in the sun. He has always loved the summer, the hot days of the year.

He has a shopping list for Rosalie. Ever-simple: tea, apples, oatcakes, cheese, tobacco. His usual fare. He drinks his tea black, strong, unadorned. He'd never liked milk in his tea even in his former life. He'd never liked milk full stop, since the day poor misguided Agnes had tried to make him drink a beaker of it. He was sick, all over her. His mother told Agnes off, roundly, severely, and poor Agnes had cried, fearful she would lose her job. There was no more milk. Agnes kept her job.

The dark-haired man and the woman, he doesn't like the look of. Nasty pair. Selfish. And Sylvia, always back to Sylvia. Why is she here? He can't find an answer, an answer that makes any sense. He had thought she was gone forever. He saw her leave that day. Heard her tell Rosalie to *fuck off and die!* He didn't blame her for leaving. He was glad for her sake that she could leave, simply up and walk away. He couldn't. He would never be able to do that. He had admired her strength. She didn't stop to wave at him as she fled the house with a stuffed rucksack. He didn't mind. She stomped off up the bumpy track, angry, crying, her movements jerky, determined – and was gone.

And later, Rosalie's guest, that idiot, gallant in his movements, wandering off up the steep track, that new woman guest by his side. There is no sign of the... menfolk. Theo raises his face to the sun, already bearing down. Glad it's so easy to ignore people, to not get involved.

So, Anthony called her a tart, in front of Antonia. Classy of him. Drunk, like Antonia said, but even so. Kelly-Marie stepping in: sensible, predictable, "nice" Kelly-Marie. Protecting Antonia. Saving Antonia's embarrassment. At least she did that.

Wandering into the kitchen, laundry out, a crisp, blue-sky day in early May. Anthony holding her phone, staring down at it in consternation. Looking up at her, so slowly. He said, his voice taut, '"L'amour est la poésie des sens"?'

Nowhere to go, nothing to be said. She made a stab at innocence but knew her face was red, her breath had quickened.
And then— 'Love is the poetry of the senses,' she said, and despite, or because of, the awfulness, because she had been found
out and she was a hopeless liar, she smiled, she actually found
herself smiling. Daniel was a prize. She no longer cared who
knew it.

'Who the fuck is this?' said Anthony and he took a step towards her. He was trembling.

'Balzac, I think,' she replied, she remembered, and she felt
glad to have been, for once, quick, the humiliator, to get this
insult in, this jibe, cruel, but she didn't know herself then.
She'd got one over on him before the relationship finally
crumbled, which it was about to do. And he glared at her,
wrong-footed, outwitted, outraged. She slumped inside, gave
in, the relief flowing through her veins like a fever. Let him rain
down his wrath, his shit, none of it mattered anymore. If he
had been more attentive— but no, she wouldn't blame him,
that would be unfair. She was bored, that was all, as he was,
and for all she knew he had somebody else too. But she didn't
know.

'I'm in love,' she said. She tilted her head up, defiant, glad
to say such gilded words. 'I've met a man and I've fallen in love
with him.'

'That poncy French teacher?'

She was surprised. 'Daniel. Yes.'

'*Him*? How long for?'

'A few months.'

'Where? When? Here?'

'No!'

He coloured then, and took another step towards her, his breath hot on her face. He raised his hand, she flinched, he lowered it. 'I am not going to give you the chance to be the victim in this. I'm not that stupid. Get out. You're both sacked.' His voice rose to a shout. 'I'm getting him out of that fucking cushy little job and you out of my house! Do you understand?'

And Antonia, almost twelve, was there in the doorway, had been there throughout, and crying, and running to Anthony. And Sylvia knew, she saw how it would be, she was out, and she wouldn't be taking Antonia with her.

As Geoffrey and Caroline disappear into the heat of this day, and Antonia sleeps her teenaged sleep, and Theo disappears into the woods at the bottom of the field, Sylvia finds herself in Rosalie's kitchen again. Rosalie, washing up, not even acknowledging Sylvia's presence.

'Well?' says Sylvia.

'I hardly think—'

'I don't care what you think.'

'You never did, Sylvia.'

'I wonder why?'

Rosalie carefully places a plate on the draining board, taking longer than necessary. How old she looks. How old she *is*. Others would see an active woman, a little frail, but... lively. Alive. Capable, still.

'Leaving here was the best decision of my life.'

'I wonder then why you have returned?'

'Antonia. That's her name, by the way. Not Antoinette.'

'I know. I was muddled.'

'She wanted to meet you. I thought it might be... good for

74

her. Will it be?'

'That's not down to me. You're the one who left. Angry. So angry...'

'You're her grandmother!'

Rosalie sighs. Rubs a thin finger across the kitchen window, leaving a mark in the faint layer of grime. 'We both know that's not true.'

'You've abdicated that role but it's who and what you are. Whether you like it or not.'

'I don't like it.'

Sylvia has no idea where to go next. Keep talking? Walk out? Leave, finally, for ever?

'Do you remember I rang you when she was a baby? To let you know you were a grandmother?'

'Yes, my dear.'

'Don't call me that.'

'What's your point?'

'You didn't congratulate me. You didn't ask who she looked like.' (She looked like Anthony.) 'You didn't ask how I was feeling. You didn't send a gift.'

'I knew how you were feeling.'

Rosalie rummages in the cupboard under the sink, brings forth a duster, a bottle of pink Windolene.

'Be nice to her,' says Sylvia. 'And for god's sake don't let Geoffrey hurt her. He's an arsehole. I caught him *kissing* her. About to kiss her. Whatever. She's... vulnerable. She has a crush on him. Do you understand?'

The smell of Windolene simmers like ashes, and Rosalie's thin arm moves round, up, down, across, reaching to the corners. Her wooden bracelets clacking together, hollow.

'And I left because I had to,' says Sylvia. 'You didn't love me then, and you don't now.'

'I don't think it wise to love anybody. Do you?'

Sylvia, tears springing to her eyes, turns, leaves. None of this is new. Her mother will never change, will forever be cold. How damaged she must be. Only the damaged can speak like that, and mean it. And she does mean it. Is *she* damaged too? Sylvia loves Antonia, that's not negotiable, it's tightly woven into her life, her existence. It is wise to love somebody. It is! What else is there?

She slumps on to the falling-apart bench on the patio, lights up, and takes three deep drags in quick succession.

Theo emerges from the woods, and slowly he ambles towards his hut, that brown, stiff-looking towel draped over his shoulder. He looks almost fresh, wearing a checked shirt, with his black corduroys. Must be his summer garb.

She is going to talk to him. He must know. He must know things she needs to know. He has been here since before she was born, always here, alive, a fixture. She'll go now, stride over, be assertive, tell him that, for once, for the first time, she wants to speak to him about things that matter. If he shouts at her to go away, she'll stand her ground. Antonia is still in bed, Geoffrey is off with that woman Caroline, Rosalie is washing windows. Let her see, who cares. And she will see, she is there, her thin arm still going round, now cleaning the lounge window, about, up, down, across, up, down, all the smears rubbed out, one by one. The sun is high, insects feverish. Sylvia finishes her cigarette, stands.

Theo goes into his hut, and closes the door.

Later. She'll talk to him later. She will read her book, sunbathe out on the lawn. Get a glass of cold lemonade. Think about all the bits and pieces she needs to buy for Antonia's birthday. Make a list. She'll be useful.

Theo likes to keep his hut tidy. He makes his bed. He puts away his toiletries in the little corner cupboard. He sweeps the floor, opens the door, and sweeps out all the dust and dried foliage. He'll lay on the grass, hat tipped down over his eyes, and he'll listen to the world.

And he lies on the grass, the patch he mowed yesterday, the bit in front of his hermitage. It's getting noisy at the cottages. The girl awkward, stuck. Not fair. He ignores the demon-sized dramas being played out. The little lives spilling their puny guts, revealing all manner of human pettiness. It's not for him, and it's easy to ignore. He recalls another time, another drama.

'When are you going?' she says, fighting tears. Good. It's about time she cried. He's never seen her cry. She's always been so cold, and distant, and utterly hopeless. But now, when he is finally going away, to forge a new life, in the city, *his* new life, she cries. It was his decision, in the end. Mother, Father, and certainly Meredith, they had nothing to do with it. He has impressed this upon himself. What is he supposed to do, spend the rest of his days on this shadowed, forgotten estate, while the world whizzes by outside, and stay with this woman, so "common", a slut, yes, a common tart (although she wears no make-up). He is doing this for Meredith, doing some of the things he couldn't do. The valley has given up all it can. He needs to go, and he will go, and she lays her head on his lap and cries, and when she begs, he can't bear it.

'You'll meet somebody else!'

'I may not.'

'You will! You'll forget about me.'

Silence.

'You've forgotten me already. Haven't you?'

'I will never forget you.'

'I don't want your empty promises, words mean nothing. Theo. Theo. What's happened to you?'

'I think I've grown up.'

'You've always been a grown-up to me!'

And the sheer awfulness of it, the realisation that she wasn't so confident, so bold, that it was all an act. It came crashing in and he knew, yet it was too late. Arrangements had been made. He could not, would not go back. He had a room in the home of his mother's stepmother's niece. He had met her, discussed the arrangements. A widow, older than him, and pretty, alone, and it was a draw, no doubt. Rosalie tired him. She had been his first, his only, up to now. But life was for living, his life was his, and she had men, others, boys, he supposed. She had admitted to it, without shame. Now it was his turn. He would go.

The second-floor flat was drab but it at least had a small balcony, outside space, so she could smoke. Maybe grow some potted roses. Tomatoes? Somewhere to dry her laundry. Anthony would keep child benefit payments, he had insisted, and yes, it seemed fair, so she allowed that. The flat had two bedrooms and the landlord gave her permission to decorate, as she had taken out a two-year lease. So she painted Antonia's room first, in a pale calm green, and bought curtains and a set of bedding. Brand new.

Anthony ensured Daniel was sacked, as he'd said he would do. Waltzed into school, not a thought for how his kicking-up of such a fuss would affect his daughter. Which it did. Most of the kids laughed at her, made crude jokes. Mr Charpentier left, rapidly. Then his wife finally left him.

He came to the flat, drunk, one evening, a week or so after Sylvia had moved in, ringing the bell angrily, three times in quick succession. She buzzed him in and opened her door to a man she barely recognised. Dishevelled, clutching a bottle of red wine, half-drank, half-drunk, waving the bottle around in dramatic fashion.

How the hell? Why? Why did she have to allow it to be discovered? He'd lost his job *because of her*. He'd lost his wife. She'd known all along, all of it, but couldn't face the humiliation. But in the end she had to go. Had enough. Stupid, stupid Sylvia.

She asked him to leave. Told him she wasn't entirely to blame. They were pretty even. Weren't they? She didn't recognise him in this mood, in this angry approximation of the gentle man in the bath, reading poetry and touching her body and mind oh so softly. This couldn't be the same man. Crying, ranting, angry.

'Where will you go?' she said, the obvious suggestion hovering on her lips. But not in this state. The aura of shame crushing her, and him, and their love, if it had ever been love, lost. Was it love? Now she was doubting even that.

'My friend will put me up. Until I find another job.'

'Where does he live?'

'She lives in London.'

And he was gone, shaking his head, turning from her. And so it would go, so it would be between them. *She*. Of course. On their second date: *Most of my friends are women. I prefer their company.*

She hadn't understood, then, she took it at face value. But, of course. Of course.

Antonia didn't like the green. It was too pale. The flat was small. It was cold. It smelled funny. She stayed one night that first month. Then she stayed no nights and over the phone (Anthony had insisted she ring) she said she didn't want to see her, not for a long time. And she had decided to leave the school and Dad was putting her into another one, better, an all-girls school. It would be a fresh start and there would be no more teasing and taunting and whispers. *Mum? It's all your fault.*

'Morning!'

She pulls down her sunglasses and it's Chris, chubby blond Chris, the doormat. She waves, half-beckons, and he joins her. She lays down her book, which she wasn't managing to read. She'd actually had her eyes shut, drinking-in sounds, and almost dropping off.

'Fancy a smoke?' he says, and sits alongside her, the bench creaking and shifting. She hopes it won't break. It's old, weather-beaten, the slats sagging. But it holds and they smile at each other in acknowledgement of this. He offers a cigarette and holds his lighter for her, then sparks up his own cigarette. The self-satisfied and rebellious fraternity of smokers settles over them.

In silence, they contemplate Theo's hermitage. She waves her cigarette towards it. 'I never thought to ask him anything about his life when I was growing up here. You don't, do you? Kids accept things for what they are.'

'As do some grown-ups,' he says, raising his eyebrows and taking a long drag.

'Yeah, well. You can change whatever you want. You're not a kid.'

'I know. Thank you.'

'Don't mention it.' What a sweet man he is. And he is a bit like a kid, seeking validation. *Come on, man! Pull yourself together.* 'Actually, thank me for what?'

'Making me realise I *am* a bloody doormat. I think I needed somebody to say it. I'm going to my sister's.'

'Good for you. When?'

'Today. Gonna pack my shit and go. I didn't bring much anyway. I never do. I don't have much.'

'What a shame. The weather is set fair for the next few days and this is your holiday.'

'It's no holiday.'

Silence. Then: 'Look, ditch the raven-haired gits and come and stay in my cottage. We have a spare room. My mother won't care two hoots.' It's rash of her, yes, rather an odd thing to suggest, even, they barely know each other, but she wants to be kind, the exact opposite of her scoundrel of a mother; and it's kind to offer, and he won't take her up on it.

'The raven-haired gits?' And he laughs, loud, with gusto. Then: 'Do you mean it? I won't be in the way?'

'Oh... Yes, I mean it. The spare room is the smallest, but it's adequate. You'd be more than welcome.'

'I won't be underfoot?'

'No. Antonia doesn't speak to me anyway. I could use the company, to be truthful.'

'But that's fucking weird!'

'Hush! And don't swear.'

'But it is fucking weird. We don't know him.'

'He's a nice man and I offered on the spur of the moment—'

'What does that even mean?'

'Without thinking it through. I'm sorry.'

Antonia sighs heavily.

'Look, it's for a few days and it will mean the poor man gets his holiday. And we can keep out of each other's way, can't we? Let's you and I go for a walk together one evening. I wanted to do that with you while we're here.'

'Walking is boring.'

Chris is getting his clothes and toiletries (*All I have in this world*) and he will take up residence in the small spare room. Sylvia won't even bother telling Rosalie, who wouldn't care anyway. Antonia will no doubt mention it.

Sylvia has taken a blanket from the huge saggy sofa in Columbine and spread it on the lawn in front of the cottage. Sun cream applied (Sylvia has to use loads; Antonia has her father's thicker skin), iced lemonades by their sides. Antonia has her mobile, Sylvia her paperback. Cushions too; and they are set.

'You were happy enough to go walking with Geoffrey yesterday.'

'That was different. He was teaching me to sketch.'

'Was he.'

They sip their lemonade. The ice has already melted.

'Oh no, look at that bitch,' and Antonia prods Sylvia, who turns to see Geoffrey and Caroline enter the gate and head towards them. Rosalie waves from an upstairs window in Rose. She must be cleaning all the windows. Neither of them notices Rosalie or her wave.

'Good morning,' drawls Caroline.

'It's the afternoon,' says Antonia.

'So it is,' says Geoffrey. 'How time flies when you're having fun.' He looks pointedly at Antonia who blushes. *For god's sake.*

And from Bluebell comes Christopher, with his bag, and a bottle of champagne.

'What's going on, darling?' says Caroline in that feigned-innocence sharp voice of hers which is already annoying and Sylvia doesn't even know the woman. But she knows enough about her.

Something prickles through the thick noon air: invisible lightning. Sylvia, slouching on the cushions, sits up. She reaches for a cigarette. Her eyes meet Chris's, fleetingly, but enough, and she nods, lights up, and takes a long deep drag. And now here's Tom, hands in pockets, following Chris.

'I'm leaving,' says Chris.

'But it's beautiful here, darling.'

'Caroline, I'm not your darling. Tom is. I'm leaving you. And him.'

'About time,' says Tom, as he stands alongside Caroline. Geoffrey, who Sylvia almost feels sorry for, takes a step away. He looks embarrassed. Everybody does. Is she the only one enjoying this?

'Yes, that's right. I'm no longer in your set-up. It's been

making me ill. It's been a disgusting time in my life and I've made the decision to end it. I'm not going to be your doormat anymore.'

Tom steps towards Chris, kicking over Antonia's lemonade as he does so, leering at Chris. 'I'll have my Veuve Clicquot back. If you don't mind.'

'Tom, actually, mate, I do mind. This is mine. I'm going to drink it tonight, with Sylvia here, to celebrate the start of my new life. I don't ever want to see you again and I won't be returning to London with you.'

'Where the hell will you go?'

'My sister's.'

'Look at you. Fat, boring... utterly fucking anodyne. I never understood what she saw in you.'

'At least he's not a cunt.' They all look at Sylvia. She shouldn't have said that. She raises her eyes at Antonia, and shrugs a mute and half-hearted apology. She takes a drag on her cigarette. They all seem to be waiting for further explanation. 'I've invited Chris to stay with me and Antonia, so he can enjoy the rest of his holiday. In peace.' She glances at Caroline, who has the front to look hurt.

Tom points at Chris. 'You're a pathetic freeloader, you know that? Sponging off Caroline. Hanging around us all the time. Good riddance to you.' And he reaches out for the bottle and Chris yanks it away, pushing at Tom, who stumbles and falls on to the blanket, now sending Sylvia's lemonade sprawling.

'Do you mind?' she says, glaring at Tom, who gathers himself from the ground, red-faced.

Silence descends. Nobody knows what to say or do. Sylvia takes a furtive look around. Geoffrey stands at a distance, bemused. Caroline is crying; Chris almost too, bless him. Tom furious, humiliated; Antonia, still sitting on the blanket amid the red-faced, lip-biting, rapidly-breathing adults. At least Antonia looks amused. *Good. Still her girl, then.* From Rose cottage comes Rosalie. She must have heard the commotion.

Sylvia glances towards the hut. Theo is laid out on his back on the grass, hat pulled down over his face, hands behind his head. He is listening. She can tell. Why wouldn't he be listening?

'Look,' she hears herself saying, 'it's simple. Chris is staying with me in Columbine. He is leaving his girlfriend – that's you, Caroline – because he doesn't like you shagging another man while he's in close proximity. Sounds perfectly reasonable to me.'

Caroline wails, turning to Tom who takes her in his arms. Antonia has sidled towards Geoffrey.

'Chris, go on in,' says Sylvia, nodding towards Columbine's open door. 'And put that champagne in the fridge.'

Caroline wails some more: 'Darling Christopher, why?' Tom steers her towards Blubell and the door is slammed shut behind them. Caroline's wails, now furious shouts, are muffled and obscure.

'Better get this blanket washed,' says Sylvia, and she gathers it up as Antonia stands awkwardly, neither helping nor hindering.

'That went well,' says Geoffrey, and he chortles. 'That Tom is a complete wanker, no?'

Sylvia can't disagree. But she won't let on. Geoffrey is a wanker too. But Chris is not and she finds him in her kitchen, putting the champagne in the fridge, as she instructed. 'We'll drink it later, shall we?' she says. 'Well done.'

Chris shrugs. 'I don't know. I didn't mean to upset her.'

'She's a drama queen. She must have seen this coming.'

'A normal person might have.'

'Yes. And you're normal, and now you're free.'

'Thanks, Sylvia. I mean that.'

And Antonia bursts into the kitchen, her smile wide. 'I'm having dinner tonight with Geoffrey and... and my grandmother.'

Sylvia peers through the window at Geoffrey's hollow wolfish form, as he stands on the lawn, looking sadly towards Bluebell with its firmly closed front door.

And Theo, eyes closed, the sun warming his face even through his felt hat. Who doesn't enjoy a good row? *A jolly good row?*

He doesn't. Hasn't for years. Never has. Yet people row, they argue, like just now, all those adults in their ludicrous pantomime, the girl, poor thing, stuck in the middle, looking from one to the other, oh yes, he knows that feeling, half-confused, half-fearful. Confused, fearful. Yes. That's how it was.

The train ride was long and hot, with no refreshments, and he was pleased to see Philipson waiting by the car. And entering the park, twenty minutes after disembarking the train, he wound down his window, Philipson politely following suit. The dark lushness of the trees cooled Theo, in body and mind, the wind whipping around his head in the Jaguar (Father's, but Philipson was trusted to drive it). The steep twisting decline to the house, and then the house itself; white, grand, pillared, home. The curvaceous lake, and beyond the house, the meadows, the woods, the track to the workers' cottages, and to her.

His life had bounded ahead. He had his new London girl-friend, his new London flat-share, his new London job. Something in an office. Even he wasn't sure what it was, but he shuffled papers and signed papers and filed papers and most evenings he took his latest girlfriend, Paulette, out for dinner, dancing; it was a high life, a city life, and he was enjoying it. Paulette was quiet, reflective, measured, even in bed. Refined. She wore a lot of powder-blue outfits. She was beautiful. He enjoyed her, but she wasn't— *but...*

As he approached the front doors he heard shouting. He entered the hallway, and Clem stormed past, growling something at him. He seemed taller, his thick brown hair sticking up on his head, as usual; a wild look in his eyes. He barged into the passage towards the kitchen and Theo heard the crash of the side door. Theo entered the drawing room. His father barely nodded, before: 'That boy will not learn! Oaf!'

'Simon, please...' Mother. Sitting on the piano stool. Theo went to her, kissed her head. She looked tired, greyer. How long had he been in London? Eight months? Things had changed.

'What now?' asked Theo to the room at large. Mother took his hand and kissed it.

His father shouted, 'Your brother is a lout!' Wheezing, red-faced.

'Simon, *please...*'

'I'm glad I came back then.'

'No Paulette?' said Mother.

'She doesn't like the countryside.'

'Pity. How long are you staying for, darling?'

'A couple of days. Sorry.'

'I've a bloody good mind to drive her and her family off my land, out of that house, and out of my employ! Once and for all!' The angry squeak of the decanter, the glug of a lavish pouring of brandy.

Mother grimaced. Theo tapped her shoulder, and left the drawing room.

'Your room's made up!' she called after him.

It wasn't until he was in his room that he realised what his father had said.

The cork bursts and Sylvia holds out two glasses.

'Cheers!'

They smell it; sip; pull the first-sip face, and take another.

'And congratulations,' adds Sylvia.

Antonia is in the bath. Already preparing for her "dinner-date".

Chris slumps into the deep saggy sofa. His tummy plump in his white T-shirt.

'You shouldn't wear white,' she hears herself saying. Too blunt. Always too blunt.

Chris examines himself. He takes a swig of champagne. 'What you mean is, get a grip, you fat slob.'

'No. OK, a bit. You're a nice-looking man and a nice man. Lots to be said for both of those things.'

'But lose the excess.'

'You've done that already! And men lose weight easily. A few runs, a bit of discipline, you'll be a stunner.'

'You're kind. And you smoke too much. You should give that up.'

'I know, I know. I love it.'

'Me too. P'raps I should smoke more, eat less.'

'That's my trick.'

They finish their first glass and when Sylvia reaches across him for the bottle on the coffee table, he kisses her. It's rather a nice kiss. Not invasive, but dry, tender. Still a shock. She hasn't been kissed for years.

'Sorry,' he says, and holds out his glass for Sylvia to fill it.

'It's fine,' she says. 'A reaction. I must feel like your knight in shining armour.'

'You do, rather.'

'I'm not. And I... I won't be your lover either. Apart from the fact it's rather too soon for you, we don't live near each other and...'

'And?'

'Nothing.'

'So you do have a fella?'

'I *had* a fella. I don't have him. It didn't work out. I think... I think my heart is broken. Whatever that means. Stupid expression.'

'I'm sorry, Sylvia. You deserve—'

'It's OK.'

'It's sad.'

'I'm used to it. Let's get drunk.'

'Good idea.'

Theo walked towards the cottages, the track steep, rocky, the loose stones treacherous underfoot, so he took to the grass. He smoked a cigarette, and wondered what he would find. The last time he saw her she had cried, and begged him not to go, not to leave her. She had got on to her knees, wrapped herself

89

around him, and he had – cruelly, he supposed – unwrapped her from his body, stood back, and left, her sobs ringing in his ears. Her words, almost true: *you will find somebody else; you won't ever want to come back; you'll forget me.*

He reached the first cottage, Rose, which was the Rawe family's home. The door was open. He heard her mother singing to herself. He tapped on the door, and Mrs Rawe came.

'Oh. You.'

'Yes, me. Is Rosalie around?'

'She's… she's…'

'She's around.' And Rosalie was there, behind her mother, and refused to look at him through her deep-set eyes, even more deep-set now. Her face looked… dowdy. Yes, dowdy. Not glowing. She'd always had country skin. Something was wrong. Again, he wondered: had he misjudged her? Misunderstood her all those months? Was it love she felt? Her flippancy and playfulness a mere protection? She'd been dramatic when he'd left. But he had misjudged her, possibly. Deliberately, possibly.

She stepped around her mother and out into the light and his insides lurched, his organs leapt and danced and landed, confused, in the wrong places. She looked haggard. Thin, thinner than ever. And all he could do was look into her sad pale blue eyes. And he was minded of Paulette, her pale blue clothes, her healthy, strong frame, her smiling face. And of course Rosalie would be thinking of her too. With a rush he realised what he had done to her. And how it should never have started; and even how his parents were right, but also wrong. But it was all his fault. And jealousy was killing this woman, he could see that. His fault.

'Would you like to take a walk with me, Rosalie? Please?'

Her mother, brazenly, considering who she was and who he was, shook her head, tutted, sighed, and retreated back into the dark of the cottage. So she knew. Everybody knew. They hadn't been as clever as they'd imagined. Foolish.

They walked for a while in silence, Rosalie with a yellow cardigan draped over her shoulders, her bare legs thin and tanned and dusty beneath her drab skirt. Her shoes were scuffed, her hair bedraggled – unwashed? – and he realised Paulette, he and Paulette, was a sham. Rosalie was not a sham. Rosalie was real, raw, she smelled of sweat and oil and hair, not Youth Dew. Yet Rosalie was youth. So young and fresh and strong. But… She didn't stop him when he yanked her towards him and kissed her. They rushed, ran, to the meadow and threw themselves down into the tall-growing wild flowers. He made her cry. Afterwards they lay on the warm earth, entwined, tired, and she slept. He cradled her. He thought about asking her what his father had meant. But decided not to. *I've a bloody good mind to drive her and her family off my land, out of that house, and out of my employ! Once and for all!*

They didn't mention Paulette, later. Nor would Rosalie say what the matter was. It wasn't only jealousy. Something else. But he couldn't – wouldn't – allow himself to think it or voice it, any more than she could bring herself to mention the name Paulette. So like everything else between them, it went unsaid.

She'd said, 'Mum? I'm having dinner with Geoffrey and my grandmother tonight!'

Dinner? Deep breaths. She mustn't over-react. 'All right.'

'Can I have wine?'

'If it's on offer, a glass, yes.'

Muttering. Stomping upstairs to "get ready".

Sylvia's not invited. But she can't say no to Antonia going, not without looking like a killjoy. The reason they are here, even if ostensibly, is for Antonia to spend time with her grandmother. It's a damn shame that bloody idiot is hanging around. Can't he go night sketching or something?

She'll cook for Chris. Something simple. She has pasta, a jar of sauce. That's her limit. Chop up a few vegetables to chuck in with it. Freezer pack of garlic bread. Cheap eating; she's had to embrace that since the separation. Her food bill is small. Half of it is spent on cigarettes and booze. Bad mother. *See, Chris, I am a bad mother.*

And it's Antonia's birthday on Friday. So tomorrow she must drive to Rowan Bay and buy a cake, some nibbles, balloons. *Balloons?* Probably not. She's sixteen, not six. Champagne, then, more champagne. She'll splash out on a couple of bottles. Although it has already given her a headache, the bottle she shared with Chris earlier. Chris is lying down in the spare room – now his room. Prosecco might be better. Certainly cheaper. Champagne can be… cloying.

She has brought Antonia's present with her, a beautiful silver locket on a delicate chain. Not cheap. All gift-wrapped and good to go. Classy, stylish, what a girl turning sixteen might like. And a thirty-quid Boots gift card. For her make-up, her "products". The locket cost over a hundred pounds. This has been the most she has spent on Antonia's birthday present since the marriage ended. She hopes Antonia will appreciate it, but it will be over-shadowed by Anthony's gifts. He always makes sure of that.

Geoffrey had better not— he'd better not *hurt* Antonia. He

doesn't deserve Antonia's company and if he kisses her (again?) she will cut his bollocks off. She will. Even if metaphorically. Should they go home, now, today? No. Antonia would never forgive her and she's already not forgiven for many other things. And they can't leave Chris on his own after inviting him to stay. That wouldn't do.

The bath runs. Antonia moves around in her bedroom, the floorboards creaking, and she opens the wardrobe, and is probably laying out various outfits on the bed. She brought so many clothes. Oh, let her have her fun, this date as she seems to be regarding it. Rosalie will be there. Nothing will happen. Not even Rosalie would...

She leaps up from the sofa.

'Hello, dear.'

    'My name is Sylvia.'

    Sigh. 'Hello, Sylvia.'

    'I want to ensure you are aware of your responsibilities. Again.'

    'What can you mean?'

    'You have invited my daughter for dinner and I expect you to... chaperone her. I think we both know what Geoffrey is.'

    'Do we? What is he, dear?'

    'A cunt.'

Rosalie appears unfazed by the word, but she doesn't like it, Sylvia can tell, there is always present in her a deep-rooted puritanical sort of disapproval. Which is ironic. Rosalie cuts stems, thrusts flowers into a large blue vase.

    'What was all the fuss about earlier?' she asks.

    'Nothing. The other guests have had a parting of the ways.

Actually Chris, the nice one, is staying with me now, if you don't mind.'

'I don't. They seem like a rather strange lot.'

'The other two are horrible. Chris is a good man. Unlike Geoffrey.'

'I have heard you, dear.'

'If my daughter gets hurt... if her feelings are hurt... I will hold you responsible. In your home, in your care, you are there to look out for her. She is your granddaughter and you owe it to her.'

Rosalie sighs. 'Look, my dear, would you like to join us? Put your mind at rest?'

'No. Antonia would hate that. Be her grandmother. Please. She is innocent.'

Rosalie thrusts another flower into the vase. The arrangement is complete, perfect. 'There we are,' she says.

YES. *YES*. That tattoo, dazzling her, although she may not have thought of the word: *dazzle*. Yet she is good at English. She's going to do it for A level. Geoffrey offers to top up her wine glass and he does so, not by much, but a little, she notices that. The red wine glints and shifts like a liquid jewel. On her plate is some kind of pinkish-grey meat, long thin green beans, and slices of potato in a white lumpy sauce. They must have forgotten she's a vegetarian. She pushes the meat around, away from the potatoes.

The conversation is weird. They talk over her head, in a strange grown-up language she can't decipher. Certain words, yes, they come into focus, but then they dissolve back into the... impenetrable?... mass of the conversation. *Priggish*.

Christopher, I think. Ménage à trois. *Good lord! Brisket. Plump. Wet blanket. Palate.*

'Antonia, is the meat not to your liking?' Her grandmother, eyebrows raised, a gentle half-smile, not really a smile. It's... mocking?

'I'm a vegetarian,' she says and her voice is too quiet. She sounds dull and stupid. She sounds like an eleven-year-old.

'Oh, you poor thing,' says Rosalie.

'I chose it. Mum's not a vegetarian.'

'That's something,' and Rosalie and Geoffrey smirk at each other. Antonia picks up her wine glass and hides her face behind it.

'Never mind, my dear. We have rhubarb crumble and custard for dessert.'

She doesn't like crumble, custard, or rhubarb.

Yesterday Geoffrey had almost kissed her. Hadn't he? Had she imagined it? She couldn't tell, now. Her mum ruining the moment, ruining her life, something she enjoys doing. Cheating on her dad with Mr Charpentier. What a bitch.

The normally cool kitchen is hot, the candles scattered around the table making the room hotter. That afternoon, yesterday, yes, Geoffrey had almost kissed her. He had. And now you wouldn't know, you would never guess. He hardly looks at her. He talks to... Rosalie... more than her. Why did they invite her over? They don't want her here. They only want to talk to each other.

She sips a bit more wine. Geoffrey tops it up, again, a little, the YES on his arm a terrible taunt. He won't look at her, and carries on talking to Rosalie, who is laughing and now getting up to "do" dessert. Geoffrey still won't look at her.

After a couple of mouthfuls of the horrible rhubarb crumble, the thick custard, and another slight top-up of wine, she endures more nonsensical words, and another hour, longer, of being ignored, or if not ignored, not included; a few questions shot at her every now and then. Questions about her mum. So she tells them everything she can think of about Mum, and Mr Charpentier, the divorce, her dad, Kelly-Marie, Mum's horrible, weird-smelling flat. And Mum wouldn't like that she was talking about her, but she deserves it, and the polite mocking faces goad her on to say more, and she isn't being ignored now, she is being heard. Yet her voice sounds small in the large kitchen.

Later: 'Time for bed, young lady,' and he gets up, and comes round to her side of the table, and takes her arm.

'Goodnight, Antonia,' says her grandmother, holding her wine glass, and still smirking, but in her friendly way. She isn't like a grandmother. Mum did warn her, and Mum was right. Which is annoying.

At the door of Columbine cottage, Geoffrey puts his hand on her waist and draws her to him, and is about to kiss her. Like he almost did yesterday afternoon. Everything swirls. She runs her hands through his hair. She hasn't done anything like that before. But he mustn't like it because he's pulled back. 'Steady on, girl!'

And then the door is yanked open, and there's Mum in the dull yellow hallway (it's the same colour as that revolting custard), looking daggers at Geoffrey.

'Here she is!' he says cheerfully.

'Thank you. Goodnight.'

And Geoffrey is gone, and Mum pulls her into the cottage,

holding her hand, tightly, and she mutters something under her breath, and closes the door, with that extra bit of effort when it sticks.

THURSDAY

Theo rises with the sun. He has, all his life. A constant. He checks his list, then walks, slowly, silently, up to the door of Rose cottage and lays the list on the bench in the porch. He does this sometimes, avoiding having to talk to Rosalie. She'll leave his groceries in the porch for him to fetch. There is no breeze this morning, just this still air, and the sun beginning its own long day. The valley will be ablaze within the hour. Already the birds are busy, the dawn chorus his alarm call. Deafening, beautiful, one of the great thrills of his life.

It was a shame about Paulette, but inevitable. In the end she bored him. The powder blue outfits, the perfect hair, the endless *dancing*. The clinical, oddly sexless, sex. Lovely woman, but not for him, and he hadn't enjoyed making her cry, but such was life. He had now made two women cry (three, if you included his mother) and he wasn't proud, but he would make amends. Not to Paulette, not to his mother, but to Rosalie. Although Paulette had stalled him, distracted him, it hadn't changed a thing. It had merely crystallised that which he already knew.

He was twenty-seven, the oldest surviving son of a well-to-do country family, he would one day inherit a beautiful home and park. He had slept with a dozen women, more, Paulette only one of his distractions. The only girlfriend. She didn't know about the other women. The others had been nothing at all, selfishly used as a means to an end, for his own gratification. He didn't even know the names of most of them and had not seen them again. Best that way.

But a lonely way, and he has felt lost in the wilderness. It doesn't matter how many women he sleeps with; if he knows their names or not; if they are beautiful, refined, fun, clever, stupid, vacuous, intelligent, vain, pretty, fat, thin, ugly, selfish, rich, poor, generous, crippled, athletic.

They are all strangers. They are not *her*. His one true wife.

He makes his tea and examines the cottages, dead for now, but they will soon be alive, pouring forth inhabitants, both permanent and temporary, into the drama and promise of a brand new day. A deer, hesitant, ghost-like, eases across the field, looking about, nervous. It disappears into the hedge.

His tea tastes grand this morning. He has put more tea on his shopping list, along with his customary oatcakes, apples, cheese; also soap, this time, and tobacco, and new boots – sturdy – size ten. She'll know what to get.

He picked up the shrill telephone. 'Theodore Fenchurch.'

'Theo?!' Mother. Stressed again. He had thought for many years that she might have been better off without Father. He was a bully, emotionally, if not physically. But of course she enjoyed the material advantages of her marriage, and he knew she had always been in it to the bitter end.

'Hello, Mum. Everything all right?'

'No, Theo. Your father died last night. Clement is taking it badly. Can you come?'

So now this summons, as he took it. This was it. He would have to return. Paulette, vanquished, his mind made up, and now this death, this death to change everything, and the excuse, if he needed one, and he did, to return, to take up his rightful place.

The park was unchanged, the lush green of it. Philipson drove the Jaguar (now Theo's, or Clem's, if he wanted it) with none of his usual composure. Was he even crying? He was, and looked rather pathetic, so Theo resolved not to notice. Philipson, stern, concentrating despite his tears, the hairpin bends in the park negotiated with skill and precision. Tears wiped away. And after the final bend, down on to the flat valley floor, they drove past the Capability Brown lake, over the little bridge, always a bump, *better take it slow*, and on to the sweeping gravel drive.

Philipson parked neatly in front of the house. The sunlight gave the house a glow: festive, rich, heavy, and substantial, a giant Christmas cake. And was this now his, all of this? His and Clem's?

He didn't cry even when Mother ran to him across the chequered hall floor, her face mottled, red, and fell sobbing into his arms. He kissed the top of her head, and led her into the drawing room, and ordered tea from Mrs Philipson. She too was tearful.

'Where's Clem?' Theo asked, after Mother had ceased her crying and was drinking her tea.

'With the the Rawe girl, I think.'

'Oh.'

'They've... become rather thick.'

Sipping his tea, he watches as Rosalie opens the door to Columbine, and picks up the list, which she scans. Then she looks up, and nods at him. He nods back. Later today, or tomorrow, his groceries will be in the porch for him to collect, hopefully with the new boots. He'll wear them in over the summer. And as he watches Rosalie shake out the doormat, he realises that these new boots are almost certainly going to be his last pair.

Chris enters the kitchen, yawning, possibly hung over. Champagne can do that. She notices, with a little smile, that he is wearing a plain dark blue T-shirt. Better. He has combed his hair, washed, shaved. He's all pink and glowing. *Good man. That's the spirit.*

'Coffee?' she says, and waves at the pot on the stove. 'Fresh and strong.'

'Yes, thanks. May I join you?'

'Of course.'

He gets coffee, adds sugar, is about to add a second, and stops.

'How did your daughter get on at the dinner?'

'I think that arsehole kissed her goodnight.'

'Are you sure?'

'He's far too old for her. I'll have it out with him later.'

'Don't embarrass her. It's… would you like me to have a word with him?'

He's right. She mustn't embarrass Antonia. How would Kelly-Marie handle it? With perfect poise and wisdom.

'No need, thanks. I can fight my own battles.'

'Of course. I didn't mean… of course.'

'Sorry, I didn't mean anything either. I can handle Geoffrey, is all I meant.'

'Sure.'

'I'm popping into Rowan Bay this morning to buy birthday things. Would you like to come with me?'

'Bag carrier at your disposal, m'am.'

She smiles. How easy he is, how nice.

'Toast?' she says, standing up.

'Oh, go on. Why not?' He taps his belly. 'Just a slice.'

She makes toast, several slices. They eat in silence, but it's not awkward, until:

'Who's this fella then?'

Sylvia glowing hot and stinging. Tears pricking at her eyes. Who indeed? She doesn't know *who* he is, only what he is.

'What fella?'

'The one you almost told me about.'

'Oh.'

They smile at each other. *I can't fool you, can I? Nope.*

'It was a ridiculous affair. Should never have happened. My husband found out, he dumped me, got D— got him the sack, and… *he* dumped me too. Went off to live with some other poor woman. His "friend". Then my daughter also dumped me. Full house. Judge me.'

'I don't judge anybody, Sylvia.'

'You say that. Everyone judges, even if they claim they don't. It's what people do.'

'Not me.'

They munch toast, sip coffee. The silence is a comfort.

'Do you still love him?'

'He's a womaniser. Terrible attitude. Women are there for the taking. Bodies. Access to sex. I thought he was better than that. I had no idea, to begin with, although the signs were there. Knowing finally he was such a man... it was one of the biggest disappointments of my life. I thought he loved me.'

'Do you love him?'

'He doesn't care about anybody.'

'Yes, yes, I got that. My question is, do you love him?'

Sylvia's tears fall. Chris apologises, rubs her arm. Offers to make more toast. She laughs.

'Toast is the answer,' she says, and wipes her face. Then: 'Yes. I still love him. Of course. Being with him was the most alive I have ever felt. The most... plugged-in. To life. To that energy that can completely pass us by if we're too careless or too unlucky or too scared. He made me feel like a new person. A new me? I didn't recognise myself, but I liked her. I *loved* her. I didn't know I was that person. Being with him brought out the best part of me. I loved him and her together. It felt like magic. It *was* magic. Do you understand?'

Chris shrugs, and helps himself to a fourth slice of toast. 'Sorry... such a pig... Yes. I do understand. I've not experienced it, of course, but it must feel... something. Really something. Try not to... lose it. You should fight for that. Womanisers can grow up. There must be other qualities in him you admired.'

Sylvia nods. 'Many. That's what's so damned frustrating.

Heartbreak aside. He... he wasn't true to himself. Not allowing himself to be the rounded human being I know he is, under-neath all the silliness.' She pours more coffee. Wishes she hasn't shared these feelings. But glad that she has. Saying it has made it real, and detached from her, distanced, not hers anymore. Like Daniel Charpentier. *Womaniser.* Words in the air, pumped out into the receiving stillness, landing on Chris's calm acceptance.

'I take it he's a stunner, this chap?'

'Daniel. His name was Daniel.'

'Daniel.'

'You mean hot stuff, as in looks?'

'Yes. Must be.'

'No. Ordinary. Average, I suppose.'

Theo slumped back in the cracked and creaking bottle-green leather chair; his mother dismayed, but not, perhaps, as shocked as he. The study clock ticked, loud, uncompromising. Theo asked Mr Shackleton to go over it again, one more time. Mr Shackleton, grave, quiet, embarrassed, did so.

Theo glanced at his mother who stared resolutely ahead, out of the window, at the lake. It was raining, hard, the whole world grey, submerged. Shifted and distorted.

'We'll have to sell it, Mother.'

'No.'

'We have no choice.'

'Sell everything? The house? The land? The cottages? We can't, Theo. No.'

'We can and we have to. Father's debts—'

She leaped up, slammed her fists on the table. Wild, retching sobs. 'Damn him! Damn him to hell! I hope he rots there!'

Mr Shackleton, uneasy, shuffled papers, putting them back into his briefcase.

'I know a good land agent...' he offered. 'I'm sure he—'

'Out of my house, Shackleton! Out! Please.'

He settles Mother in the drawing room with tea, scones, cream, jam, which she simply will not be able to eat, but she will try. He goes off in search of Clem.

When Mother... no. Helena. Why not use her name? She was a person, after all, and they had never been close, not like how it was with her and Meredith, or even her and Clem – when Helena announced she'd had enough and was packing her bags, flitting from the wardrobe to the chest of drawers and back again, he wasn't entirely surprised. And the... friendship... before Meredith. Before her *wedding*. And Theo had no idea who the man was, no idea at all, he'd never met him. Her first love. Her only love, and she was going back to him. She was free. The estate? *Do what you have to. I'll not return.* If it couldn't be hers... why did he think she stayed, all these years? Putting up with the bullying, the boredom, the grumpiness, the revolting eating habits, the snoring? Meredith made life bearable, but he had to *die*, Theo; your brother died.

Theo knew this. His existence had become the reminder.

Later, a car arrived. Helena said goodbye, and when she hugged him, she said, "I'll be in touch, I'll sign anything that needs to be signed," and Theo felt the force of her coldness, and if he never saw her again, he wouldn't be sorry. She hugged Clem, who stood motionless in her arms. Neither son waved as

105

the car left. They stood alone, listening to the sound of the engine fading away through the trees, and then silence, save for the birds.

Theo turned to Clem. 'I have to sell the house. Everything.'

'I know.'

'What will you do?'

A shrug, a look to the ground. 'I don't know. What will you do?'

'I don't know either. Go back to London I suppose once I'm finished here. Look, Clem, I'll do it all. It's my responsibility.'

'Of course it is.'

'I know you were close to her. I'm sorry.'

'What do you know?' And he smirked, and scoffed, and left Theo alone on the gravel drive, the house looming huge and white and empty behind him.

'Geoff?'

A sigh, a resigned smile. 'Yes?'

'Leave my daughter alone.'

'She's almost sixteen, isn't she?'

The urge to slap him passes. She'll keep her composure. Somewhere in this human being there is compassion. 'Please. She has had a tough time.'

'That's your fault, is it not?'

'That's irrelevant. We're talking about my daughter, not me.'

'What goes around, comes around.'

She fights another urge to slap him. 'It's her birthday tomorrow and it would be great if we could... could all celebrate with her. In a *friendly* way.'

'Of course.'

'So we understand each other?'

'Perfectly.'

'In that case would you and Rosalie join Antonia and me... and Chris... for champagne and cake tomorrow? About four o'clock? Afternoon tea.'

'Delighted.'

'Let Rosalie know, could you?'

He calls out, 'I say, Rosalie, we have an invite for a champagne afternoon tea tomorrow. Antonia's birthday "do".'

And Rosalie calls back, 'Lovely! Oh, Sylvia, Antonia told me you're off into town this morning?'

'Champagne won't buy itself,' says Sylvia.

'Could you pick up a few things for me while you're there?'

In the car, windows all the way down ('You don't use air con in Devon!'), Chris beside her, a cigarette in her hand, a cigarette in his, the chat is easy, the laughter flows, and for a moment she's happy, happy again, it all comes back to her, that lightness of existence. Daniel made her feel this way. Chris is not Daniel, and she wouldn't want him to be. Good company though, but there the comparison must end. Chris is a lot less complicated. Because she doesn't love him, of course. Could never love him, not like she loved – loves – Daniel. But this ability to be happy in the company of somebody else is a new discovery, and it's a relief.

She parks the car in the top car park and they amble down to the shops, chatting about small things. But they're OK, the small things. Chris wants a black T-shirt, two or three, even. Black is the new white, he jokes. Sylvia has Theo's list.

They buy a cake from the bakery. Champagne and Theo's tobacco from the mini-supermarket. Rosalie's things. Also flour, butter, milk, clotted cream, jam. They buy a sixteenth birthday card, and balloons, from the newsagent; and Sylvia considers the postcards. Should she send another? No. What's the point? She has embarrassed herself already, possibly even caused trouble. It had taken her a few minutes on her mobile phone to track down his address. She doesn't know, can't know, what her postcard may have precipitated. But the dream is over. If Chris can walk away from what had kept him trapped, that enmeshment, she can do the same. It has to be done. Disentangle, put that heavy burden down, lighten the load. It's her choice. It might be nice to walk faster, freer, through life, untether her heart from this weight. Longing isn't living. She's been fooling herself and thank goodness for Chris and his uncomplicated ways and the stark fact that she doesn't love him. Life is easier without love. And she shudders. She's not like her mother! She is not. Life *is* love.

Chris is a useful cake-carrier, but they don't find any black T-shirts. This isn't a black T-shirt kind of town. It's all seaside and postcards and fishing boats and big black cliffs and sun on glinting sea, joyful shouting, holidays. Hard to believe she grew up here, in this alien place.

They find boots in the outdoor shop. Size ten. Sturdy.

'We found these boots,' says Sylvia, proffering the box.

Rosalie takes them, thanks her.

'Champagne tomorrow at four, don't forget,' says Sylvia. 'I got cake too. I'm going to make scones. Must go and hide it all now so Antonia doesn't see it.'

'I'm afraid I don't have a gift for her.'

'Of course. No gifts expected. Join us for a drink. Smile. Say grandmother-ish things. Give her something of yours, if you like. Shall I take Theo's stuff down to him?'

'There's no need. I leave it in the porch. He fetches it himself early in the mornings. That's our way.'

Too good an excuse, an opportunity, to heed "ways". 'I'll pop it down now. He's at home, I see. No worries.'

Sylvia approaches the hut. He turns to look at her. 'Be off!' he shouts, and she stops, taken aback. He used to shout at holidaymakers like this. But it's gruff, not aggressive, and she advances a step or two closer. A bluff. A gruff bluff.

'I brought your stuff,' she says. 'See? Apples. I got Pink Ladies. I hope you like them.'

He nods. Breathing quickly, shallow.

'Can I— may I sit with you? Please? I want to talk to you.'

'Leave me alone.'

'No, I won't. Sorry. I need to talk to you.'

He stares, droops, and he nods. She sits down on the log beside him, puts the bag on the ground at his feet.

'Boots?' he says.

'Damn, I forgot them. Rosalie took them in. Shall I...?'

'No. I'll fetch them myself.' He speaks differently to how she had imagined. A bit posh, when she'd assumed country bumpkin.

'Do you know who I am?' she asks. Always get to the point.

'Yes.'

'Good. Because I don't. Will you tell me?'

For a long time he says nothing. He rifles through the bag

of groceries, and shuffles into the hut to put things away in the cupboard. He comes back out. Sits next to her on the log.

'Ask away,' he says, then he speaks, quietly, answering her many questions. He tells her almost everything, slowly, simply, he tells her all she needs to hear. What happened, why it happened, when it happened.

'You're my *uncle*?'

'Yes. I was there when you were born. Me and the midwife, in Rose cottage. The midwife was so disapproving... I'll not forget that. Rude, even, she was. Rude about me being present and about Rosalie being unwed. I lied, you see. Said I was the father. That midwife looked at me like... she thought I was strange.'

'And you love Rosalie, still? That's why you do all this?'

'I let her down. I swore to protect her, and I have, as much as she'll let me.'

'Love is terrible, Theo.'

'Not always. Is it your cross to bear? Love?'

'Of course. Unrequited, I think. I don't actually know. There's a man... Daniel is his name... ' and now she tells Theo everything, *everything*. More than she told Chris. She tells Theo of her longing. She tells him about how much she misses life. She tells him how she has hidden away and closed herself up and how only Daniel, of all the hundreds, thousands, of people she must have met in her life... Only Daniel touched her. Truly touched her, the human being named Sylvia Rawe. And how it's not romance she craves or misses, romance is trivial fluff. And she sent him a sign, an invitation, she let him know in the face of humiliation that it's not over for her and never will be, even though it is... and she tells him about Antonia, the sadness of that situation, the disconnect. The one other person she truly loves, besides Daniel. Daughters and lovers. One daughter, one lover. Her "loved ones". And how their mother-daughter connection is lost, broken, but must be fixed. It must! And Theo gets it. He nods, tears in his eyes. When she has finished, quietly crying, he takes her hand.

'Give love every chance it deserves. It's the only thing we have. All else drops away. Meaningless. All the *things*. Teacups and jigsaw puzzles and cars and books and jewellery and holidays and money. None of them mean a damn thing. If you love somebody that's the real richness of life. You love your girl. So your mother didn't love you? That's her loss, and it's her great loss. You love your girl and she loves you, despite what you think. And this man, this Daniel, you're right to give him another chance. If he makes you feel this much, you should try again. Allow yourself to try. Find out for sure. If he's no good, so be it, don't waste your time on him ever again. Unresolved love is the worst thing. I live it every day. Rosalie will never forgive me for not being your father. I don't forgive myself. I love her more than life and I failed her. I won't fail her again. Love destroyed me, that was my destiny. But it can do the opposite and it's always a gamble and it can be a terrible thing. But life is terror, the knowledge our life doesn't last forever. It's unbearable and the one thing mitigating against that is love. I would take terrible love over no love at all, and that's what I've done. You will triumph with your daughter, with Daniel too. But you have to be brave to triumph and it takes guts, and you have guts. Don't be scared, don't fear the one thing that matters.'

'OK.'

'Thank you for my groceries.'

'I'll remind Rosalie to put your boots in the porch.'

'Thank you.'

'We're holding a little tea party for Antonia tomorrow. She's sixteen. Will you join us?'

'No.'

'I wanted to invite you anyway.'

'That's kind.'

'All right, I'm off. Thanks, Theo. "Uncle" Theo. I'm not sure how I feel about you, but I thank you for your honesty. You told me more than she ever has.'

Theo nods.

'All those rumours,' she says. 'They're mostly true, aren't they? Truer than people realise.'

'I've not heard any rumours.'

They smile.

FRIDAY

The cake has kept fine over night and it will keep cool all day in the darkness at the bottom of the musty wardrobe. It's already hot at half past six. She sits on her bed, blowing up balloons. Should have bought a pump too, damn it. She's hopeless at blowing up balloons. The smoking. She should stop. She ties another, bumps it away and watches it bounce soft and light, and it lands, gently quivering, on the dressing table. What to write in the card? She never knows. She doesn't want to be trite and sentimental. She wants to be real. *I love you, so proud of you on your sixteenth birthday.* True, if uninspired. Of course she is proud of her. The only child she would ever have, ever love. And, like her, an only, but unlike her, loved, loved properly. Not perfectly. Love is never, can never be, perfect, and there is comfort in that. But Theo was right. Love deserves every chance.

She'll bake the scones later, as late as she can get away with. Thank goodness the kitchens are so cold in these cottages.

Hard to believe so many years had passed. It was time he visited, and he wanted to take Angela, he did, he knew he ought to take Angela. She wore the beautiful pearl ring he had bought her last month. Unusual choice for an engagement ring. Unusual girl, Angela. Unpredictable, and not always fun. Sometimes too much fun. He probably shouldn't marry her. He'd been sucked into it, after a swanky lunch in Claridge's, with Helena. He hadn't seen his mother for a couple of years. She looked older, fatter; happier? Living with her first-and-only-love must agree with her. Helena took to Angela. And Theo loved her. She was perfect. And in a rush of euphoria after the tipsy lunch he'd proposed to Angela and she'd said yes; and now... now he was going home. He was going back. Clem would pick him up at the station. He told Angela he was visiting a sick relative, boring, no need for her to join him. And she announced she and her mother were commencing wedding-frock-ideas-shopping and she would be busy. What did he think of silk? Perfect with pearls?

He left London on the train that afternoon, and if he had known then that he would return but once (to pick up the rest of his things and quit his flat, and his job, and Angela), once only, for the rest of his days, he might have said goodbye properly to his affianced, apologised for wasting her time, if not breaking her heart; he would have sauntered through Green Park one more time, along Piccadilly, a last visit to Hatchards. But he didn't. He simply hopped on a train, bound for the west country.

Clement looked wild. Frightening. Gaunt, his eyes huge. His hands were dirty, black under the nails, cuts on the knuckles. He drove unsteadily, too fast, erratic. His brown hair still stood up in its wild clumps and tufts. He smelled unwashed.

114

'Clem?'

'What.'

'All right? Are you?'

'Never better.'

Silence. A pheasant ran out, dithered. Clem braked. 'Stupid fucker!' The pheasant jerked one way, then the other, a strange panicked dance, and finally with a great deal of flapping and fussing it bounded over the hedge. Clem roared through the gears, the car straining.

'You could slow down,' said Theo.

Clem slowed, sneered, shook his head.

'What?' said Theo.

'Who d'you think you are?'

'What does that mean?'

'Lording it up in fucking London. Coming back here like a fucking king. What's it been? Ten years? Why you bothering?'

'Nine years. It was my home too.'

'And?'

'I wanted to see how you're getting on.'

'I'm doing fine. They pay me and I live in the cottage. I'm a tenant, a servant, on my own fucking land. It should have been mine. Ours.'

'Which cottage?'

'Columbine.'

'It's not ideal. We had no choice—'

'Selling it like that. Don't bother asking me. Bullying Mother into it.'

'Nobody bullied anybody! Clem, come on. There was no choice. At least you didn't have to deal with it.'

'I should've. I would've kept it. Somehow.'

'No, you wouldn't. It was impossible. It's done now. Why don't you leave? Start again somewhere else?'

'Where's your latest flame, anyway? Miranda, is it? Funny, you never have brought one of your fancy women down here. Not once. Wonder why?'

Theo felt his face redden. Clem, he was… sharp, sometimes. 'It's not Miranda.'

'I can't keep up with you, Romeo. Got a photograph?'

'For Christ's sake.'

'Meredith wouldn't have fucked this up. He would have kept the house.'

'Would he.'

Clem floored the accelerator as they entered the park. They raced past the lake, past the house, stayed on the road that continued through the park.

He stamped on the brakes and brought the car to a jerking halt by the wall. The cottages still looked the same. The park looked the same. You would never guess it now had a flashy new owner; a businessman from America. A glamorous, rarely-seen wife. He couldn't blame Clem for his bitterness.

'Seriously, why don't you leave?' Theo said as they got out of the car.

Clem gave him a look so strange, so unnerving, and Theo shuddered inside, and looked away, busying himself getting his bag from the boot.

He glanced in the windows of Rose cottage as they passed. No sign of life. Years since he had seen Rosalie. Had he missed her? Only if he allowed himself to, which he rarely did. Convincing himself he didn't need her or want her. It could never be.

They were on different... levels. Different planes. He had his London life, his glamorous wife-to-be, his mysterious pen-pushing job. Rosalie was not of that world. She was basic. Lower-class, he supposed he meant, but he didn't want to frame it in that way. But she was. She was common. He wasn't. *Too young, Theo.*

'Mrs Rawe died,' said Clem as if talking about an ancient tree, fallen. He pushed open the door to Columbine.

'When?'

'Last winter. Got ill, all of a sudden. Then she went.'

'And you didn't think to tell me?'

Clem shrugged, smirked. Columbine smelled of dogs, dusty rugs. 'You'll have to sleep on the couch. The bedrooms are full of my things. Stuff that wasn't fucking auctioned, anyway. I had to steal my own belongings.'

'You should have let me know!'

'Should I?'

'How's Rosalie taken it?'

'Like you care!'

'Of course I care.'

Clem shook his head, laughed a low bitter laugh.

'What's she doing with herself now?' asked Theo.

'Scrubbing. She's a scrubber.'

That was enough. *Oaf!* 'Don't be facetious, Clem.'

'She cleans up at the house. Char woman, like her mother. Now the Philipsons have gone, it's all down to her.'

'And Mr Rawe?'

'Drunk most of the time. Took the death badly.'

'Oh, poor Rosalie. Her mother.'

'You ever hear from ours?'

'Occasionally. I met her for tea in Claridge's not so long ago.'

'How nice.'

'It was a little awkward, but it was all right. She met Angela.'

'*Angela*...? What the fuck happened to Miranda?'

'There never was a Miranda.'

'Oh. So who am I thinking of?'

'Shirley?'

'All right, what happened to Shirley?'

'Not much. It fizzled out.'

'You always say that.'

'Is Rosalie at home?'

'Don't know.'

'Does she work on Saturdays?'

'Sometimes.'

'I'm going to see if she's at home. I'd like to extend my condolences to her and her father. I wish you'd let me know.'

'Mr Rawe?'

Rose cottage was dark in the hallway, bright in the kitchen. That big window. The table was covered in breakfast things. He found Mr Rawe snoring quietly in the lounge, mouth open. The smell of drink was unmistakeable. No point in trying to wake him. He crept up the stairs. 'Rosalie?' he called.

She wasn't there. No sign of her in any of the bedrooms. The place was a mess. He could do with a cup of tea, but he knew he should seek out Rosalie first. So he walked up to the house. The rhododendrons were out, blooming with that sickly pink-purple colour he had never much cared for.

Oh, the house! The wedding-cake pomposity. He marched across the gravel, and boldly rang the bell.

And it was she who opened the door. Gaunt, like Clem, pale, drawn, a blemish on her cheek. A bruise? Surely her father didn't—?

And she collapsed to the floor, sobs racking her, and he helped her up, held her to him, and then they were in the drawing room, that most delightful of rooms, sunlit, the French windows open to the terrace. He seated her in a plush velvet chair by the window. All the furniture was new. Of course. Her sobs subsided, but she didn't look at him, couldn't.

'Shall I ring for tea?' he asked, and then realised why he shouldn't. Rosalie laughed, but like Clem's, it was low and bitter.

She stood. 'I get the tea.'

'I'm sorry. I didn't think. Stupid of me.'

Together they went to the kitchen. She was spring cleaning, alone in the house. The owners were due back from New York in two days and had asked her to ensure the place was spotless. She was the only help now, other than a team of cooks they hired; "caterers" as they called them, who came in when needed. The family were of course informal, being American, and resident for a few weeks in the year. It was their holiday home, really. And they wanted to turn the workers' cottages into holiday homes too. She and Dad, and Clem, had been asked to make their own arrangements. She could keep her job. But she had no home. Dad couldn't cope since Mum died. Hadn't worked for ages. Clem did it all now.

They took their tea back to the drawing room and slowly

they drank it, one cup, two, Theo pouring. How tired she looked, this woman. Not a girl any more, and he was not a boy. Hard to believe they were both in their thirties already; where did their twenties go? His spent in London, living it up, cushy meaningless work, cushy meaningless girlfriends. Rosalie was stick-thin, worn out, and this was no life for her, none at all! Angela, her assured vitality, her confidence, her made-up face and smart hair-do, her mini-skirts and strong legs. Paulette, her powder-blue outfits, her utter blandness. Shirley, her neat black bob, her white skin, her caustic laugh. And Miranda, dear god, Miranda. There had been a Miranda: beautiful, and without doubt the most promising of them all. But even she had to go. No good. Not—

Rosalie could never be bland and they were kissing and un-dressing and the hydrangea bushes were tap-tap-tapping on the glass and—

'What's this?' Her pale thighs were bruised, inside, purple and grey and yellow-tinged. Storm clouds. He touched one of them with his thumb, softly. Rosalie turned away from him. 'Rosalie? What's happening to you?' Surely *not* Mr Rawe? No. It couldn't be. Drinking was one thing, drinking in grief. But harming his daughter? No. Yet... yet there was always some-thing amiss with the man. Mrs Rawe was her daughter's pro-tector, and from what, Theo had never troubled himself to wonder. He looked again at her face, the blemish across her cheek bone, indeed a bruise. 'Tell me.'

Rage. Rampant. Blind and furious. Guilt. It will never go away, now and forever.

Clem was in the shed, chopping logs. The thud of the axe,

the split of wood.

Theo stood in the doorway, looking down on his brother, his wild and furious brother; both of them, of course, wild and furious, in their own ways. Meredith, never wild, never furious, lost to them, and he would have saved everybody.

The veneer of his London life stripped away, split from him. The city civilisation, a meaningless thing, after all. Nothing to him. He could have stayed here. *He should have stayed*. Or – taken her with him, married her, set up home. She always was his wife, and all the others were mannequins, window-dressing, attempts to avoid the simple truth of his life. He was born for her. He could not escape. And now he would do what needed to be done.

'Clem?'

He looked up, red-faced from the exertion of chopping the wood. He knew immediately, Theo saw that. Clem stood up straight, defiant, the axe in his hands.

Theo cast around the dim shed, the dark corners slowly coming into focus. The axe was too obvious, too bloody. He'd be caught, hung. Would he? Not any more. They were stopping all that. Hanging. And coiled in the corner was a rope, an ammonite about to come back to miraculous life. Theo calmly reached down for it. Clem breathed heavily.

Theo said, and Clem could not refuse: 'Come with me. Now.'

He remembered the tree, they used to climb it. Nobody saw them go up there. Mr Rawe was dead to the world in Rose cottage, Rosalie was up at the house spring-cleaning, the American owners were in New York, and not due back for another two days. Mrs Rawe was dead. Father was dead. Meredith was dead. Mother, too, almost dead, in that peculiar way of hers. Clem didn't seem to understand what was about to happen. They faced each other.

'You beat Rosalie. You force yourself on her. You rape her. You hurt her.'

'You can't rape that bitch. You should know that.'

'You are vile. No brother of mine.'

'What's it to you?'

'I love her.'

'Love. Pull the other one. Like everybody else around here, you had a go on her.'

Theo thumped him hard, across the cheek. A bruise. Damn. Could ruin everything. But this *cunt* of a brother! Clem, on the ground, dazed. Barely conscious. Theo set up the rope, quickly. He wasn't sure how he knew how to do it. Paulette had once described it to him, in a rare dark moment. Her uncle committed suicide by hanging, and Paulette and her mother had found him, had tried to get him down. (Not so bland after all.) A noose, a strong noose. Clem, struggling to stand, dazed, watching Theo. The noose was ready. How to get Clem into it? He thumped him again, on the side of his head, knocked him flying. Couldn't resist. His hand throbbed. But Theo lifted him, lifted his own brother, hoisted him up, whispered to him, *You're worthless, you want to die anyway, you have no compassion, no idea of what love it, you are stupid and evil. You're the devil. And if you don't do this, Clem, I will report you to the police, and to jail you will go, you rapist, you batterer. Forcing yourself on my Rosalie! You couldn't cope with jail, Clem, you couldn't. So take this instead. Escape.* Theo hoisted him up, groaned, shouted out in the effort, forced Clem's head through the

122

noose; Clem feebly struggled, then stopped, still and silent. Must have thought about the alternative. *Better to die here, my lad, than in a prison cell.* Theo panted hard, holding his brother's full weight. All he needed to do was let him go. Clem was still, quiet, heavy. Theo must have thumped him harder than he'd meant to. He lowered his body, gradually letting go the weight. The noose tightened. Clem's eyes were wide and staring, entreating.

And Theo let go, finally, stumbled back, two steps, three. And Clem came alive, he thrashed and gurgled, he hands clawing at the noose, but he couldn't do anything, it was too tight on him. And Theo sat down in the long cool grass, took a blade of it to chew, and watched his brother die.

Clem was still, eyes open, unseeing, then and forever. It was right. It was just. Suicide. The poor, tragic, displaced Clement Fenchurch. He couldn't cope with the death of his father, his mother leaving, the loss of the family home, the bleak shame of being a tenant, worse, a servant, and finally the cruel order to vacate even the cottage, and the pressure became too much, and he finally took his life, on a hot June day in 1966, found later by his distraught brother, Theodore.

And that will be the story; and of course the rumours will follow, but there will never be any proof or knowledge, only tales. He could see it all. And after the funeral he'd return to London, terminate that life, collect his few belongings, and he would return to the park, to Rosalie, and, no matter what, he would never again leave her.

*

And on the first day of July, he entered the park for the last time. The American owners were sorry, so very sorry, for Theo's loss, and if not ashamed, alarmed. They had decided to allow Rosalie and her dad to stay in Rose cottage, and the other two would be holiday lets, and Rosalie was to manage them, that would be her job, as well as be the daily cleaner at the house. An arrangement to suit everybody. And yeah, why not, sure, Theo could stay... there would be things he could do. Work. Now that Clem had passed away.

He'd left Angela distraught. Had she loved him too? Not playing at love, like he'd assumed? The pearl engagement ring flung back at him, a plate smashed, and her furious sobs resonating all the way down here on the train. He was a heartless bastard. Careless with women. But not any more. There would be no more women. Only her.

Sylvia and Chris, smoking on the battered bench on the patio. Tom comes through, carrying bags. Face like thunder.

'Are you leaving us?' asks Sylvia, smiling sweetly. Chris looks away, to the ground, trying not to laugh.

Tom ignores them and strides in a tall manner to his car, slings the bags in the back, and returns. 'Yes, we're leaving,' he says, stopping in front of them. 'Caroline is taking all this rather badly.'

'Caroline should think more carefully before messing with people's lives.'

Tom nods. 'You're right. Of course. But she's not boring, you see, unlike others. She lives life to the max. She knows what she wants.'

Chris colours, takes a long drag on his cigarette.

Sylvia says, 'I've always found "boring" people to be the ones who have a lot more going on underneath than you can ever imagine. People who know how to keep themselves hidden. Those who "live life to the max" as you put it are actually the boring ones. And people who "know what they want" tend to be selfish dickheads. An observation of mine.'

When they drive off – Caroline wouldn't look at them, nor say goodbye – Sylvia high-fives Chris. They light up celebratory cigarettes.

Rosalie and Theo walking, up to the flower meadow.

'I need to sit down,' she says, and he helps her to sit, and sits beside her.

'You know it can never be, don't you?' she says after a while. 'There is never going to be a you and me. I know what you're thinking.'

'Why not?'

'Because I don't want it.'

'Yes, you do. You begged me not to leave.'

'And you left.'

'I made a mistake. Can I put it right now?'

'Right? Who are you to talk about what's right?'

'I'm sorry, Rosalie.'

'Theo, I'm pregnant.'

'Oh, god. Clem?'

'Yes.'

'Do you need my help? We could go to London, get it seen to. Nobody need ever know.'

'Seen to? No. I'm keeping it.'

'You want to keep Clem's baby?'

'Yes.'

'But you're not... I can't see you as a mother.'

'That's nice.'

'I'm sorry. What I mean is... what I mean *is*, are you sure you want to keep this particular baby?'

'Yes.'

'Conceived in force?'

'He was kind, sometimes. Everybody is.'

'My god, Rosalie.'

'I am keeping it. I'm not going to be a good mother but at least this baby will have a life. I'll give life and if I do nothing else right, I will have done that.'

'What about your work? How will you work?'

'I'll take her with me when I clean the house and she can sleep, or play, whatever it is babies do. Nobody cares about unmarried mothers these days, especially Americans. They're modern. Dad knows. He doesn't care either. But he never has.'

'She?'

'Yes, she. This is a daughter. I'm going to call her Sylvia.'

The champagne bottles sit proudly on the kitchen table, the vintage crystal glasses, smeared with age, patiently waiting. Balloons float and moon about, bumping into one another softly. Silly idea. They get in the way. Why did she bother? Antonia's gift sits next to the champagne, with one envelope containing the Boots gift card; another, her birthday card. Antonia said she would open them when the others were there. A lonely gift for a girl. They shouldn't have come to Devon, not this corner of it anyway. She should be in Newquay, Cornwall, somewhere loud and brash, for youngsters. Not here. The scones turned out all right. They sit, humble, on the plate, next to bowls of clotted cream and jam.

What has Mum bought her? Something cheap, always is. She understands why. Dad has all the money. Sometimes she wonders if it's his money that Kelly-Marie is into. Dad isn't good-looking, she supposes; or even kind, sometimes.

'Where *is* Rosalie?' says Mum, and she is cross, always in such a bad mood.

'And Geoffrey,' says Antonia.

'Yes, all right, and Geoffrey.'

'Shall I go and chivy them up?' says Chris, standing in front of the open fridge door. His face is pudgy and pink.

'I'll go!' says Antonia, her black body-con dress clinging to her. It's restrictive. What's the word her grandmother used? *Plump*. She is plump. The cake sits *plumply* alongside the champagne, under a big dome thing.

She'll have a tiny slice. She'll have one scone, to be polite. Mum isn't plump. Neither is Kelly-Marie. Nor was that Caroline. At least she has gone.

'Yes, OK, give them a knock, Antonia,' says Mum.

She sees that old man, Theo, coming through the gap in the hedge, heading for her grandmother's cottage. Should she speak to him? No. He looks cross. Are all the adults cross? Her grandmother isn't. Geoffrey is, often, but in a cute way. She heads into the cottage.

'Hello?' But it's a whisper in the hallway, a coldness and a stillness taking her voice, and the stairs are there, in front of her, and she knows not why, but she is creeping up them, one

127

at a time, in stealth. And then the noise. From behind the bedroom door, a strange noise, like a bird dying. Antonia's hands sweat, she can't hold on to the banister. Have they forgotten? Where are they? Geoffrey must be in his studio. She approaches her grandmother's bedroom door. It's shut, utterly closed on her. The dying bird sound continues. It's her grandmother, it must be. Is she ill? Should she go in? Should she knock? She sounds... what is the word... delirious. Delirious! A fever? It must be horrible to have a fever on such a hot day. She puts her hand to the door. Slippery on the brass handle. Slowly she twists it. A footstep downstairs. Her mum? Can't she even be trusted to do this? The door gives. Another footstep, on the stairs, a long way behind her. She screams. And the world nosedives, it spins, and she opens the door wider, against her instincts to slam it closed. And Geoffrey leaps up from his knees, and her grandmother's thin legs close, and he wipes his mouth and stares at Antonia, but he says nothing as she sobs. And she turns to go back down the stairs, but she is drawn into Mum's arms, Mum is there, holding her, and Chris is panting up the stairs, and that old man, Theo, he's half way up too now. They all stare into the room, Rosalie now sitting on the bed, pulling her frock down. Smirking. And Geoffrey reaches out, shakes his head, and closes the door on them.

Antonia helps her load the bags into the Fiat. Sylvia tells her it will be all right, let's get home, I shouldn't have brought you here. Antonia telling her it's not her fault, and they hug, again, and Sylvia sees she is wearing her new necklace. She doesn't know when she opened it, but it looks beautiful on her. And Chris, dear Chris, to-ing and fro-ing, bringing bags from the cottage and not knowing what to say, but helping anyway. Eating a scone. Antonia crying, bewildered.

She shouldn't have brought her here. Whatever was she thinking? Some things can never be fixed, they are irretrievable. Some people are born helpless and cruel. History repeats itself. And she allows herself a glimpse of that moment, finding her boyfriend and her mother naked together, in *her* bed. The humiliation and shock, her mother's blasé attempt at an apology. There was no apology.

Her Fiat is small and Antonia's bags need careful arranging to fit them all in. Sylvia is hot, tired, and she wants to go home, to her flat. It's poky, drab, and miserable, but it's hers; hers and Antonia's, when she wants to be there. It's fine, all fine.

Chris brings her the two unopened bottles of champagne.

'One each,' she says, and takes one, and wedges it in the boot between bags.

Geoffrey emerges too, from Rose cottage. Looking, for once, abashed. He beckons Sylvia to him, who ignores him.

'Please,' says Geoffrey.

She goes to him. 'What?'

'I must apologise. To Antonia. I know she won't want to speak to me so I'm telling you. Rosalie and I have had... this ... *understanding* for years. I genuinely didn't... it wasn't my intention for Antonia to discover us in the act. I forgot the time. I suspect your mother didn't. I think she knew perfectly well. Hoped...'

'Yes, probably. She's got form, has my mother. She's a disgrace. That's why I left. Do yourself a favour and leave too, today. She's poison. Maybe you have a chance with Caroline. I suspect Tom will be "out" soon enough.'

'You think?'

'Yes. Goodbye, Geoffrey.'

Theo wanders up to them. He looks tired, worn. She finds herself saying. 'Why don't you leave? Come and stay with us. Get away from here, from her, once and for all.'

And Theo smiling, kindly, shaking his head, and he will never leave, despite everything, no matter what Rosalie throws at him, he belongs here and will die here. Sylvia won't ever return, and therefore they will not meet again. And that's why she came back, not for Antonia, not for Rosalie, but for Theo. This is what she'll tell herself.

The car is loaded, all done. So now it's goodbye, and she hugs Theo, a big, strong, warm hug, the first and the last. He smells of woodsmoke, soil, hot dry grass, sweat. Antonia, too, hugs him, and he kisses the top of her head, and whispers something to her. Antonia's face brightens. Sylvia won't ask what he said. Not her business. Chris shakes Theo's hand, and then the three of them get into the car, Chris insisting on going in the back, even though Antonia offers to, and Sylvia starts the engine and backs up, shuffles the car around, reverse, forward, reverse, forward, glances down at the gear stick, looks up.

And there he is, ambling down the rocky and uneven track towards the cottages. He stops, waves, and she stares.

'Mum!' says Antonia.

Sylvia gets out of the car, hears Chris ask, 'Is that—?' and Antonia's excited 'Yes!'

Sylvia stands and looks at him, as he stands and looks at her, stillness, a moment, a crystal moment. Then she walks, a

130

step, two steps, as he melts into a run down the slope towards her, and she calls out 'Daniel!' and they are almost upon each other. She thinks they may kiss, embrace; but they don't. A foot, two feet, between them. Space. Always that gap. His face is... she has to look away, to the ground, for a moment. She can't bear to look at him.

'I got it,' he says, and takes her postcard from his pocket. 'I got it. I was scared. All along. A fool. I've never met anyone like you—'

'Daniel?'

'Let me finish. It frightened me. You frightened me. I don't fall in love, you see. I don't. I never loved my wife, not in the way she wanted me to. I don't believe she loved me. Love is...'

'Terrifying.'

'Yes. And rare. Isn't it? Our kind of love? But I did fall in love with you, and I didn't know what to do.' He reads her postcard: "L'amour est la poésie des sens." You are right. You are right! Sylvie, I'm sorry.'

She reaches across the space and takes his hands in hers. His hands are warm. 'Look, Daniel, after all that happened... I need to take this slowly. Four years, darling. Four long hideous years. Antonia... I need time to fix things with Antonia.'

'I can wait. I will wait for you. As long as it takes.'

'Really?'

'Really. But are you leaving?' They look towards the car. Antonia and Chris are staring at them, agog. Sylvia smiles.

'I'm afraid so. But Antonia is going to Corsica for a couple of weeks with her father in August. Why don't we... shall we meet up then?'

'Yes. Please.'

'You came all this way…'

'I was summoned. I came.'

'Your… girlfriend?'

'Not my girlfriend. My housemate. Landlady, that's all. It is the truth. She saw the postcard first. She told me I should come.'

'I see. OK. But I have to go home now, Daniel. I'll see you in August.'

'August.'

And they are gone. He won't see them again. But he is glad they came, his family. His niece, and his great-niece. Nice pair. Good people. He wishes them well. That other man, the artist, is still here. But perhaps he'll leave too. Soon the sun will set, and rise again. Rosalie too will rise again in the morning, as will he, and they will carry on in this way until they die. It will be soon. Frailty has crept up on them both. She will never change. Neither of them will. Are they victims or perpetrators? He's never known. He knows she is vulnerable. And mean. And cruel. And strong. So is he.

And Clem? He'd been right, in some ways, about Rosalie. His father had been right. *Loose morals. Slack behaviour.* She has no conscience. Psychopathic? No idea of how her actions affect other people. She is incapable of love. Other than him. She loves him, in her twisted way. He knows that much, if nothing else can be known. She never loved Clem. Poor Clem. Poor Rosalie, poor, pathetic, damaged Rosalie. He can't imagine the loneliness. If only Meredith hadn't died. If only Sylvia had been his child. If only he had murdered Clem. Poor Clem *nothing*. Thug. His evil brother. *Oaf!* Unforgivable. He'd wanted to kill him, of course. He'd never felt fury like that. But in the end, he'd found him, hanging, he'd cut him down, cradled him, cried, raised the alarm.

But he prefers the other story, the rumours. The idea of himself as a cold-blooded murderer. At least he'd told Sylvia half the truth.

He sips his tea, strong, no milk, no sugar, as the blackbird begins his song. It's the evening of a June day, the heat of summer turning in on itself.

AUTHOR & PUBLISHER NOTE

The idea for this story came to me about ten years ago and it's been "on the needles" for most of that time. I wrote it slowly, while doing my freelance editorial work and running my indie press. I started to submit *The Hermit* to agents in August 2021, just after moving house. It felt like the right time.

I guess it's a difficult sell... over the course of six months, twenty agents turned this novel down. Among other reasons, I heard that the novel was too short and too literary. I heard good things too: my writing was engaging, original, charming. I'm grateful to those who sent me a rejection. Knowing is better than not knowing.

I reckon there is more than enough room on the shelves for short, original, literary novels like this one apparently is. After all, they don't take up much space. I agree that 33,000 words *is* on the short side for a novel. But is it literary? And if it *is* (too) literary, is that now a *bad* thing? And what does literary even mean? To me, literary describes writing that has been worked hard on; thought about carefully; edited, and edited, and edited again. Artistry is involved. Perhaps literary means "low concept". I really don't know. But I take a lot of care over my work, so if that makes it literary, I'm in.

The Hermit is a story I wrote because it felt like it had something to say. I wrote it in my style, the only way I know how. I gave up submitting at the twentieth agent and decided, again, to go it alone. But I've been running LWB for several years and there isn't much I haven't learned, often the hard way, about editing and producing a book.

Sadly, in June 2023, I made the decision to stop publishing books by other writers. The pressures of running an indie press became too great. I will however continue to write and publish my own work. My fifth novel is on the way...

Louise

August 2023

LOUISE WALTERS BOOKS...

...was the home of intelligent and beautiful works of fiction. I published in most genres, but all my titles had one aspect in common: they were brilliantly written.

Further information about me and my books can be found on my website:

louisewaltersbooks.co.uk

LWB SUPPORTERS

All the people listed here took out subscriptions and in doing so helped me enormously as a publisher. I'm forever grateful to them all for their support of my indie press and my authors' books.

Heartfelt thanks to:

Claire Allen
Edie Anderson
Karen Ankers
Francesca Bailey-Karel
Tricia Beckett
JEJ Bray
Melanie Brennan
Tom & Sue Carmichael
Liz Carr
Penny Carter-Francis
Pippa Chappell
Eric Clarke

Louise Cook
Deborah Cooper
Tina deBellegarde
Giselle Delsol
James Downs
Jill Doyle
Kathryn Eastman
Melissa Everleigh
Rowena Fishwick
Harriet Freeman
Diane Gardner
Ian Hagues
Andrea Harman
Stephanie Heimer
Debra Hills
Karen Hilton
Henrike Hirsch
Claire Hitch
Amanda Huggins
Cath Humphris
Christine Ince
Julie Irwin
Merith Jones
Seamus Keaveny
Moon Kestrel
Ania Kierczyńska
Anne Lindsay
Michael Lynes
Karen Mace
Anne Maguire